■ □ ■ □ ■

THE LOSS

Writings from an Unbound Europe

■ □ ■ □ ■

VLADIMIR MAKANIN

THE LOSS
A Novella
and
Two Stories

Translated from the Russian by Byron Lindsey

NORTHWESTERN UNIVERSITY PRESS

EVANSTON, ILLINOIS

Northwestern University Press
Evanston, Illinois 60208-4210

Originally published in Russian under the titles *Utrata* (*The Loss*) in *Novy Mir*,
no. 2 (1987); "Klyucharev i Alimushkin" ("Klyucharyov and Alimushkin") in
Nash Sovremennik, no. 2 (1977); and "Kavkazkii plennyi" ("The Prisoner from
the Caucasus") in *Novy Mir*, no. 4 (1995). English translation copyright © 1998
by Northwestern University Press. Published 1998 by arrangement with
Vladimir Makanin. All rights reserved.

Printed in the United States of America

ISBN 0-8101-1639-1 (cloth)
ISBN 0-8101-1640-5 (paper)

Library of Congress Cataloging-in-Publication Data

Makanin, Vladimir.
    [Selections. English. 1998]
    The loss : a novella and two short stories / Vladimir Makanin ;
translated from the Russian by Byron Lindsey.
       p. cm. — (Writings from an unbound Europe)
    Contents: The loss — Klyucharyov and Alimushkin — The
prisoner from the Caucasus.
    ISBN 0-8101-1639-1. — ISBN 0-8101-1640-5 (pbk.)
    1. Makanin, Vladimir—Translations into English. I. Lindsey,
Byron. II. Title. III. Series.
PG3483.2.K27A25 1998
891.73'44—dc21   98-15526
                                    CIP

■ □ ■ □ ■

CONTENTS

■ □ ■ □ ■

ACKNOWLEDGMENTS

THE COLLEGE OF ARTS AND SCIENCES OF THE UNIVERSITY OF New Mexico supported this project by its award of a research semester. Research was also supported by a grant from the International Research and Exchanges Board, with funds provided by the U.S. Department of State (Title VIII program) and the National Endowment for the Humanities, and by the Center for Post-Soviet and East European Studies, The University of Texas at Austin. None of these organizations is responsible for the views expressed. The Eugene M. Kayden National Translation Award given to the translation in manuscript was an honor with implicit long-term encouragement. The translation benefited from thoughtful readings and valuable suggestions by Mary Ann Szporluk and Robert P. Gordon. Vladimir Makanin gave freely of his time for interviews and consultations, and the collaborative work with him was a major reward of the endeavor. Tania Lindsey was my constant source for information, interpretation, and encouragement in all possible ways.

B.L.

TRANSLATOR'S PREFACE

VLADIMIR MAKANIN WAS BORN IN 1937 IN THE SMALL CITY of Orsk in the southern Urals. His father was an engineer, his mother a teacher of Russian, and he was the first of four sons born to the family. His father's parents, landowners and members of the nobility, had been killed during the Bolshevik revolution; his mother's pedigree, on the other hand, was staunchly proletarian: a close uncle was a decorated Red Army commander with clout in the new regime. In the mid-nineteenth century, Ukrainian poet Taras Shevchenko served several years of exile in Orsk for "revolutionary activity," and even recently one resident characterized it as "a remote city of the penal colony category." It lies in a valley at the confluence of the Or and the Ural Rivers. In traditional geography, the Ural is the boundary between Europe and Asia. Across it begin the vast steppes of Kazakstan and, in fact, prisons and punishment camp sites populate the otherwise sparsely settled plains all around. The provincial capital of Orenburg is an overnight train trip to the west, Moscow more than a day and a half away.

The Makanins first lived in workers' barracks near the plant just outside town where the father was employed. Several American engineers who had come to Russia on contract to build factories and mills under Stalin's plan for rapid industrialization of the Urals lived with their families nearby in new apartment houses built specially for them. When they eventually moved to American-style bungalows, the apartments were freed up for their Russian colleagues. Now virtually surrounded by the industrial area of Orsk, the house at 10 Dostoevsky Street is sturdy and architecturally handsome despite its losses to time and neglect. A former neighbor still lives there and well remembers the Makanins and their oldest son, Volodya.

Makanin was a super achiever who excelled early at chess, became a city champion in the sixth grade, and was known as a "wunderkind." As a boy he learned about losses and no doubt about coping with them. In 1948, in Stalin's postwar wave of terror, Makanin's father was arrested and accused of sabotaging his own plant, which in fact he was trying to repair. The proximity of the gulag worked in his favor, making it possible for the family at least to know where he was and to try to intercede. Makanin recounts how his uncle donned his patriotic medals, took his civil war gun, and went to the Orsk prosecutor's office and demanded the father's release. His case was then reexamined, and he was released in a relatively short time. But the meager provisions the family had during this period, which coincided with a famine in the Urals, took its toll, and Makanin's youngest brother, a two-year-old, died.

Mathematics came easily to Makanin and to his brother Gennady, who was only a year younger, and the boys also shared a love of literature. Gennady even wrote poetry. Both got accepted into the highly competitive Department of Mathematics at Moscow State University. But the Urals, rich in legend and known for the independent-mindedness of their inhabitants—a quality probably nourished by their very distance from Moscow and central Russia—were to have lasting impact on the writer, who has turned often to his native region for material.

After graduation Makanin remained in Moscow as an applied mathematician in a military weapons lab, then as an instructor. But the time was the early 1960s, Khrushchev's cultural "thaw" with its relaxed censorship and westward cultural turn was under way, and the young mathematician was attracted to literature. The "youth prose" popularized by Vasily Aksyonov and others at the new journal *Yunost'* was at its peak, and Makanin's autobiographical first novel *The Straight Line* fit the genre. Based on his experience in the weapons lab during the Cuban missile crisis, it mixed sincere socio-psychological analysis with the poignant lyricism of a provincial young man's loneliness and self-discovery in the deceptive world of the big city. Makanin ambitiously submitted it to *Novy Mir,* where it attracted the attention of Aleksandr Tvardovsky, the legendary editor and prime mover of "the thaw" in literature, who liked the novel, but thought it not "mature" enough for his journal. Instead, he interceded to have it accepted by the lesser but then prominent liberal monthly *Moskva.* Its publication there in 1965 happily coincided with the first Russian publication of Bulgakov's *Master and Margarita.* The issue of the journal was passed hand to hand and, according to one estimate, eventually read by two million people.

Makanin gave up his career in mathematics in favor of writing, a courageous decision in view of the fact that he had married and now had a young family to support. Again with Tvardovsky's help, he won admittance to the Soviet Institute of Cinematography, where Andrei Bitov, a writer with whom Makanin often has been compared, was a fellow classmate. For his diploma Makanin turned his novel into a screenplay, and it was made into a successful film.

Just as Makanin's career took off, Khrushchev was deposed, the "thaw" ended, Tvardovsky was ousted from *Novy Mir,* and politically "ambiguous" works like Makanin's were rejected by the now cautious editors of the central journals where literary reputations were made and maintained. He managed to survive as a writer by publishing occasional books of stories with new works added, but the vast sea of Soviet books, often distributed at random, was what Makanin has called a "fraternal grave" of little-known writers. His only story to break through the journals' overwhelmingly gray mediocrity throughout the 1970s was "Klyucharyov and Alimushkin," published in *Nash Sovremennik* in 1977. This story, considered by many critics to be one of his best, seemed to slip in, as if its highly polished satirical and philosophical ambiguity had dazzled the politically watchful editors themselves. But this was an exception to the pattern. His novella *The Outlet* (*Otdushina*) was accepted and in proofs at the journal *Druzhba Narodov* when it was canceled, presumably for deviation from the principles of socialist realism. Moreover, the Soviet copyright agency refused to give an eager French publisher translation rights.

While by the early 1980s Makanin had established a following within a narrow circle of liberal readers and critics, it was *The Forerunner* (*Predtecha*), a novella first published in 1982 by *Sever,* a small, courageous journal in the provincial city of Petrozavodsk, that brought Makanin to the forefront and initiated continuing critical attention to his work. The novella just happened to touch a political nerve of the period and even provoked a negative reaction in the official communist newspaper *Pravda:* it portrayed an aging faith healer whose mystical powers seemed to function at times, then abruptly failed. The topic related poignantly to Leonid Brezhnev's fondness for Dzhuna, a "healer" from the Caucasus, who, according to rumor, had begun to influence government policy. Makanin's complex portrayal was appealing from both political and literary points of view.

After Brezhnev's death in 1983, Makanin's long exile from the central journals ended, and one critically acclaimed work after another appeared as his much delayed recognition grew. Here was a writer who embodied the spirit of the freer new period—one who writes against the grain, challenges orthodoxies, experiments with narrative point of view, and who maintains a strict, even silent independence, an approach usually associated with Western culture. Until the advent of glasnost under Gorbachev, such qualities were impermissible in the Russian literary world.

Refusing the traditional role of prophet so often demanded of a Russian writer, but continuing to explore new parameters by mixing essay and fantasy into a sui generis postsurrealistic mode, Makanin has continued to diversify his writing in the 1990s. *The Escape Hatch* (*Laz*), translated by Mary Ann Szporluk and published by Ardis, propels Makanin's perennial protagonist Klyucharyov, a reasonable and responsible but unremarkable man, into a futuristic Russian world of mass hysteria and chaos, where he must make crucial moral choices. *Baize-Covered Table with Decanter* (*Stol pokrytyi suknom i s grafinom poseredine*), awarded the Russian Booker Prize in 1993, examines the psychological and historical sources of Russian social fragmentation and the alienation inherent in Soviet "comrades' courts," again with Klyucharyov as an intellectual Everyman. In the now uncensored but ever intense, combative world of Russian literature, Makanin's long-awaited new novel *Underground,* serialized in *Znamia* in 1998, appeared as a major and predictably controversial event. But whatever the critical stance and readers' reception, now so diverse, surely no one doubts that his voice has become one of the primary ones in Russian literature.

"Just what are the characteristics of this voice?" a new reader may well ask. "He seems elusive, but he's been writing a long time." Two aspects of Makanin's total authorial voice dominate his writing. One is the predominance of intonation over opinion or advocacy, and this intonation performs on several scales. Quizzical, ironic, and skeptical, it is the tone of a man on a quest, but also of a writer who cares deeply about his characters, even as he believes that ultimately they alone can make a difference within their own conditions. As a writer he cannot intercede or make changes. The second important feature is Makanin's insistence on allowing room for a Bakhtinian polyphony. The structure of his fiction does not favor one voice over another, even if among his narratives' personae some must have larger roles than others.

Makanin's use of authorial voice relates to what many long-term Makanin readers see as his most characteristic trait—his distancing of himself from "problems," whether national or global. For a nation long educated to a think of the word *writer* as synonymous with prophet, teacher, and even social activist, this comes as a shock and has been interpreted by some Russians as a sign of indifference. A helpful approach to this detachment may be to see his characters as players in a chess match, deeply engaged alternately in complex strategies of attack or defense, but unaware that the outcome probably will be a draw. As a writer who was first a mathematician, he prefers philosophical permutation or reordering of components to final conclusions. The space and possibilities of perspective between two or more points interest him, not defining the points themselves. His compositional structures are frequently bipolar, almost Manichaean in their division between inscrutable but powerful forces of light and dark, right and wrong, myth and reality. Only his depiction of children, who appear regularly in his works, is devoid of binary shaping: they provide his clearest images of outright goodness and even wisdom; however, they often are condemned to arbitrary, fateful suffering.

Makanin's relationship to his readers is also important. Few writers are as trusting and confident of readers' intelligence. In a kind of silent partnership, he supplies the material and the form, the reader provides the interpretation. He invites us to witness in a thoughtful but dispassionate way the contests he presents: his characters are unusual but not extraordinary people, often individualistic outsiders in conflict with a conforming crowd; conflict is provoked by the nonconformist. "Closure" and any "lessons" drawn are strictly up to the reader. Preferring to pose the right questions rather than provide answers, among Russian writers Makanin's affinities are with Turgenev, Chekhov, Platonov, and Trifonov rather than with Dostoevsky, Tolstoy, or, among contemporaries, Solzhenitsyn and Rasputin. Makanin prefers song to sermon. The stirring passage in *The Loss* when the relatives at a reunion start to sing is an example. It's the only way to settle their old differences, to clear their consciences and assert their spiritual selves.

I've chosen three works that are different from each other, but in combination present some of Makanin's best, most characteristic writing. They are also three works that have generated much critical comment, and they happen to come from different periods. "Klyucharyov and Alimushkin" (1977) is the beginning of a cycle of short novels that explore human relations, mainly triangles—friends, lovers, spouses —and focus on the conflicts between ethics and the individual ego. *The Loss* (1987), with its popular legend of the Urals fused with a search for meaning and identity of the self, is one of several works, beginning with *Voices* in 1979, in which Makanin uses alternating narrative styles to create an intricate montage of expression that would break down barriers among myth, fictional narrative, time, and epistemology. It is also one of Makanin's most clearly autobiographical and personally expressive works. "The Prisoner from the Caucasus" (1995), often cited as one of the best Russian short stories of recent years, attracted both critical and popular readership in a way few recent works have, owing both to its timing—it appeared at the height of the recent war in Chechnya—and its immediate intertextual connections to classical works by Pushkin, Lermontov, Tolstoy, and numerous minor writers of the nineteenth century. With its disturbing contemporary twists to the romantic Caucasian adventure tale, the story lends itself to multiple interpretations on philosophical, cultural, and political levels.

As a prose stylist Makanin freely mixes contemporary, casual Russian with poetic and biblical modes of the language. This great lexical range gives a distinct ring to his prose. Occasionally a particularly laconic irony may imply a subtext not immediately accessible to an American reader, and intonation may be the only key to a set of possible meanings. While these stylistic features lend a unique imprint to his writing, they also constitute a formidable challenge to the translator. In trying to preserve these qualities I have sought equivalents rather than any strict correspondences in meaning. Also, I've tried to keep a natural flow of language so that any traces of the process of translation would be as invisible as possible. My usually inseparable priorities have been to assure that the reader receive an accurate English version of these texts but at the same time hear without distortion the vital and intelligent voice that is Vladimir Makanin's.

Byron Lindsey
Albuquerque
January 1998

■ □ ■ □ ■

THE LOSS

■ □ ■ □ ■

THE LOSS

I

EVERYONE KNEW THAT PEKALOV WAS A DRUNK AND WAS BROKE and that naturally his project all along had been utterly stupid, just as it continued to be. But still the bastard grabbed everyone who came along by the sleeve and bellowed, "Well, boys, who's coming with me? Ya know I'm digging a tunnel under the Ural River!"

And again he hollered, "Under the Ural itself!"

People in the tavern had gotten tired of it, but since Pekalov continued to yell, Pekalov's foreman, nicknamed Yaryga,* at first gestured to him, then just covered his mouth with his hand, as if to say, "Shut up, knock off the noise, it's not the time." (Pekalov jerked, tried to bellow something out, but Yaryga held him tightly.) By now people had even started pointing to the door: just get out of here!

They did leave, but at the door Pekalov, staggering drunk, bumped into a mirror and, while it didn't quite fall, the blow sent a tiny crack winding through the glass, and everybody eating and drinking in the bar shouted to them as they left that from now on Pekalov should be served only in the entryway, that neither Pekalov nor, much less, Yaryga was to be let in any farther than that.

---

*In tsarist Russia *yaryga* was the lowest rank of police officer. In the Urals and Siberia it became a term for a drunkard.

"And this is no time at all for you to be blabbing, Pekalov," Yaryga reprimanded him.

They walked out toward the river. Pekalov kept stumbling. ("Oh, no," he cried out. "Oh, no!") He fell into the sand on his knees, got up, and moaned again that he was in a bad way. Pekalov was carrying the vodka; Yaryga, the freshly smoked ham.

The day was warming up. Yaryga, lowering his voice, continued, "Because once again, Pekalov, we've got some news—another poor boy's been laid to rest."

"Oh, Lord."

The dead man lay right beside the tunnel. His red hair stuck out unevenly in tufts and patches of blood had dried on his face. His cheeks and eyes were caked with sand. No one had shown the decency to fold his arms across his chest, the devils. He was now the second one to be struck down. Wasn't it two too many? "Well, how'd he die?" Pekalov asked, and just as before, the men explained hastily and indifferently that in the darkness someone had hit the poor guy with a crowbar, either by accident or to settle some score. "What do you mean darkness? I gave them money for candles. It can't already be used up!" And, of course, they answered Pekalov by saying, "Yes, it's all used up." And the actual candles? Well, they would drop them, then step on 'em as they stumbled around in the narrow passageway. "What's got into you today, anyway? Don't you believe us?" Their explanations were muddled. Shaking as with a fever, they couldn't tear their eyes away from the vodka. They were huddling around Yaryga, not Pekalov. For while Pekalov gave the signal to start, Yaryga was the one who actually poured a glassful out to each man. Downing his portion, the man would beg and plead for more, but Yaryga would send him back to his labor.

"Now, lad, go and dig out some more earth, " he would say. Or simply, "Go and dig." Or flatly, "Move on!"

After that, the men, all fugitives, would be out of sight,

deep within the mouth of the hole, and for a couple of hours, sometimes as many as three, they would dig on without complaint. The digging went smoothly. But then they would get out of sorts. Out of some twenty fugitives working in the tunnel, only Yaryga could go show himself in the little country town. For the others it was better to sit around and drink right here—at a distance. As thieves and rapists they did their digging only out of hopelessness. They dug in forward positions as pairs, one striking his pick to the right, the other to the left. Then they would change places. In the tight space of the tunnel they had to bend low, hunch over. Behind the diggers stood one or occasionally even two shovelers in a line, and they would pass a load of earth from one to the next. While the clang of crowbars and scraping of shovels resounded, Pekalov went up to one then another of the men and whispered, "Who killed him? Whatta you think?" With a shrug the answer was, "I don't know." They worked on as the candles burned low. The place was damp, the light was dim, and Pekalov winced when he imagined how the red-haired man had been killed. What was the reason for such a sinister and senseless act? The most frightening thing was that if such a killer got going he wouldn't stop. He would quietly kill and kill again, until there would be few left in the tunnel and those would be in a state of terror: that would be the killer's sweet reward.

Bending low, Pekalov squeezed himself between the men, not only hindering their digging, but also trampling on the candles.

"Stop screwing around!" one of them yelled, as if not recognizing Pekalov in the darkness, and he kicked him toward the men who were shoveling. "Hey-hey-hey-hey!" a hefty man barked out, and grabbed Pekalov by his shirt and pants and tossed him out of the way. This was something fun to do. Finally, tired of being pushed about, Pekalov made his way out of the tunnel. He shook off the dirt and sat down beside the dead man. Here was somebody feeling no pain.

An ant was crawling across his face—from his cheek over to his forehead, then to the other cheek, which was covered with a layer of dried blood. The dead man himself didn't trouble Pekalov that much. Mainly, it meant that now he had one man fewer to work for him. This one had been alive; now he was dead. Nothing could change that. The matter of money bothered him a lot more. Pekalov had boasted and tried to show off, pretending that he still had some money, but this could last only for a while.

In the course of the next two days he lost Alyoshka. Besides whatever hopeless cases and riffraff that came along, he needed someone who knew at least a bit about the job, and for that reason Pekalov had hired and come to value the short, blond-haired little guy, who had been chased away from everyplace else for his rampant drunkenness. But by now, Alyoshka was afraid of a cave-in. He had downed a lot of vodka in a short time and fallen asleep right away. It turned out that he lay right next to the murdered man, and they looked alike: the one sleeping, the other dead. One was sprawled out here and the other over there. Suddenly Alyoshka's wife, one of those women that men hide from, appeared from out of the brush. Even she didn't realize that the man stretched out next to hers was dead, and jerking on Alyoshka's collar, she pulled him up and started yelling, "Get home! Home! You'll sleep it off there. You stinking drunk!"

She was wearing a nice-enough jacket and wore a red kerchief around her head. Pekalov was about to intervene, but looking as if she'd like to tear him to pieces, she waved him away. She could give him a real wallop; up against her Pekalov was a weakling. Collaring Alyoshka, she pushed him, punched him with her fist, and pulled him by the ears. "I was bad off already. Why did I have to go marry myself a drunkard?" she moaned as she dragged him off.

Alyoshka stumbled along as she led him away, but finally

he roused himself and broke loose, leaving half of his shirt in her hands. "Big drunk!" she yelled as she walked off. "You might've found yourself some real boss and learned a trade!" And, naturally, she then began to give Pekalov his due. "Degenerate! Disaster means nothing to you!"

At the noise the tipsy little work crew scrambled out of the tunnel. Pekalov told them to dig a grave for the dead man, and two of them carried him off by his arms and legs into some distant bushes while a third clambered into the tunnel and dragged out the shovels they would need. "Boys, don't forget to return the shovels to their place," Pekalov yelled to them, and they guffawed. Pekalov's remarks were always obvious and unnecessary to them.

Yaryga began to herd the gang back into the hole. "It's time, my boys!" He also called to Pekalov, "Put away the vodka!"

The sun by now was blistering. The huge jar with the remains of the vodka stood in the shade, covered with a damp cloth. Coming across it, Pekalov put the jug in his store chest and locked it up immediately. Here he had to keep an eye out, keep close track of things.

Hiding the key in his pocket, Pekalov slapped a mosquito on his neck and suggested to the still sleepy Alyoshka, "You ought to go in the water. Take a dip!"

"Not a bad idea," Alyoshka answered.

The two of them swam around, spouted water about, and every once in a while glanced at the other side. The shore was far away. "I wonder when it'll be that we won't have to dig any deeper. You s'pose that soon as we get halfway across the river we'll be able to dig just straight ahead?" Pekalov kept asking.

Alyoshka answered with an air of authority, "First let's get halfway across, Pekalov. Then we'll talk about it."

When the gang of fugitives and bums had put in three hours of work and came out for a smoke, Pekalov and Alyoshka went underground. In the dark at the very pit of the tunnel, Alyoshka used a sharp testing rod to probe the ground under his feet, and Pekalov held the candle. Alyoshka tested the ground at every half-step.

"Hear what rock there is under us? We can't break through any deeper."

"What about going higher?"

"Any higher and the river will collapse on us."

Pekalov started laughing. "Don't be afraid. Even a kid would see that in fact we'll pass through the space between solid rock and the river."

But intent on his testing, Alyoshka kept probing with his rod. "It's clear that there'll be a cave-in. I'm telling you, shithead, that we're gonna drown like rats."

Already on edge, Pekalov punched him right back in reply. He didn't like it when the locals called him names; every miserable drunk picked it right up.

Alyoshka grabbed him by the collar. "You fucked-up little cheap trader! You raise your hand once more on me and I'll rip you up with a knife!"

The candle went out and, holding back his temper, Pekalov had a smoke in the darkness. "Okay, take it easy! It's no big deal! Hit me, go ahead and hit me in the face, okay, but why fly off—going for a kni-ife?" he joked.

When they had made their way out, he yelled to the crew. "Off to work with you! And if Alyoshka tries to scare you, don't believe him. You deadbeats listen to me. I've figured it all out. We're going to slip under the river like through the eye of a needle."

Alyoshka kept silent.

But Timka let out a howl. As punishment for stealing and squirreling away some vodka, Pekalov had refused him any for the whole day. "The bottom's settling!"

Timka kept constantly swimming to appease his raging thirst for some vodka. With rocks in his arms to keep him down and holding his breath, he would let himself drop to the river bottom, just above the tunnel, then pushing up he'd swim to the surface, then go down again, as if he were dancing with a rock in his arms. Timka yelled like a fool that on the bottom there was mud and stuff, and that the mud was sinking right underfoot, but when Pekalov scoffed and glanced over at Alyoshka for support, he was silent, as if he even believed the fool.

"The bottom's settling!" Timka kept hollering.

And right away the drunks sitting around on the bank started grumbling. "Where're you trying to send us off to, Pekalov? You wanna ship us off to the grave?"

It was as if for the first time the thought had come to them that a cave-in might happen and a flood in the tunnel would drown them all. "Hey, men, what's this noise? Don't tell me you're trembling out of fear for your own hides?" Pekalov gave a false little laugh and tried to get their courage up. He himself was scared. He had gotten distracted and didn't immediately grasp that it was all a ploy, that the men weren't all that afraid, but what they really wanted was for him to increase the vodka rations. No matter how desperate, these men now had begun making faces and acting temperamental. They had seized their moment. And Pekalov had no choice. That evening he doubled the vodka ration. This time Pekalov and Yaryga brought food and bottles of vodka from the tavern.

Then Pekalov called Alyoshka aside and asked him straight out, "Have you taken it into your head to leave?"

"That's right."

"You're a weakling, man." Pekalov suddenly got angry. He let his voice break, and whispered, "Go off to your screaming woman, let her console you! Get out of here!"

He didn't even pay Alyoshka what he had coming and that made a double savings.

Down on his luck and at a loss for what to do, Pekalov was stuck in this little country town. He was a drunk and nothing more: no money, no reputation, no conscience. He merely drank, for no special reason, listlessly and without gusto. He was a nobody in every way. Nastya, a soldier's wife, meant nothing to him, just another woman.

"Look, Nastya, I keep thinking . . . ," Pekalov started a palaver. "Many, many years will pass, see, Nastya, but will it surprise people that even in our days it was a sweet pleasure to have some drinks in bed? Whatta you think, will it?"

Leaning up on the pillow Pekalov poured himself some vodka, and for her a splash of red wine. Half-reclining, they drank up, then he lit a cigarette and smoked, relishing it. He chuckled as she modestly drew the blanket around herself.

"What are you wrapping yourself up for in such heat?"

"I'm ashamed," she said softly.

From chattering Pekalov switched easily to moaning. He had started thinking about the tunnel crew, which kept shrinking.

Suddenly he broke into a drunken sob. "They're running off, Nastya. They'll all run away on me . . . Not a goddamn thing will work out."

"Okay, it'll be all right."

"They'll run away . . . "

"It'll be okay, I said. That's enough. Let's cuddle."

Even when she threw back the blanket, he went on crying. He was like a baby when he got drunk.

Left without even one man who understood the job the least bit, Pekalov put up a bold front and blustered about, but at the end of the day a loud din of voices rose from within the tunnel, and when Pekalov headed in to see what was the matter, he ran into several of his drunks quickly pushing their way out. A leak had been discovered. One of the diggers had suddenly felt a burning sensation. The drop of water that had fallen from above was actually cold, but it had seemed scalding to him. "Brothers! It's dripping!" he yelled, and then a panic ensued. Pekalov tried to stop them, shouting and trying to assure them that this was some wild, trumped-up story, but they knocked him down, trampling over him as he lay shrieking. Out of the darkness, one of those remaining in the tunnel yelled to him. "You just step over here yourself, then you'll believe it!"

Trembling, Pekalov crawled ahead, wedging himself through, and he, too, felt a scalding drop of water on his forehead. It was still dripping. Drops were falling here and there.

Now they all headed for the exit, Pekalov along with them. To let them go now was unthinkable. A chill wafted from both the river and the land. Rain clouds were gathering in the evening sky. "Such a genius!" Pekalov shouted out. "Hey, it's dripping! Look, water drips from the sky, too!"

But nobody wanted to work. "We'll wait till morning. Then we'll see what how it looks." They didn't even take a look at the sky. But, of course, they hinted that Pekalov shouldn't scrimp on the vodka. "Pour a little, come on— pour some," they said. Pekalov promised them whatever they wanted. He was still shaking.

Yaryga also argued with them. "The earth runs in layers," he said. "We're on a soft spot now and that's why the river's dripping through, but farther on it'll be hard again. Come on, men!"

But they stood their ground. "We'll see in the morning."

The sprinkle of rain ended, giving way to a muted sunset. When Pekalov walked past the little road where the soldier's wife lived, she was already out in the vegetable garden. All bent over, Nastya was digging around in the damp beds. Pekalov gave a little whistle and she looked around, but he had already walked by. She just caught a glimpse of him.

He came to his own little shack. Not only were the walls weathering, but from all sides this house's past life was being eaten away by age, poverty, and neglect. Still, it was home. He glanced at a portrait of his father. A successful man. His brother, too, they said, was doing well in Astrakhan. But for him, a ne'er-do-well, even digging a hole didn't come easy.

But yeah, if it could be done, what a beautiful thing it would be: to go to the other side of the Ural and take a stroll! Pekalov didn't think beyond this "stroll." He didn't have any idea why he was digging this tunnel, why people should want to "stroll" there—or even *where* it might actually be possible to walk. Through the swamp? Leaving the door open so that Nastya could come in while he was gone, Pekalov set out to see Salkov, a rich peasant who lived nearby.

"Wouldn't you like to buy my old sticks of furniture?" Pekalov asked right off as he walked in.

"No."

Salkov didn't know the details of what and how, but he did know that Pekalov was a louse, that he was down and out, and that from somebody like that you can buy more than furniture.

"How about buying half the house, hey?" Pekalov asked, himself now trying to hook him.

"Half of the house?"

From there the conversation got going, but soon it came around to the price, Pekalov, reversing himself, said, "Half the house won't do. I'll sell the whole house at once, so just buy it. How about it? Wanna take it?"

"What about the money?"

"The money, up front." Pekalov opened up and said what he wanted. "The money immediately; the deed, at least tomorrow."

"I'll buy it."

They haggled a bit, then called a man in to be the witness, after which Salkov found the ready cash and laid it out. Ah, what a rich man! After he had given him the money, Salkov asked, "Are you really leaving? Going maybe to join your father and brother?"

"Exactly. Going to my dad and brother. They've got a little something going there."

"Good thing to do, my boy, you're doing the right thing. There you'll make a turnaround in every way. People 'round here are no count, unbelievably worthless, but there, you'll get on your feet!" Salkov sang his praises until Pekalov left. But as soon as he slammed the door behind him, Salkov naturally thought, "This fool, this louse will make a turnaround only in the grave. There everyone lays straight."

Pekalov sent a boy off for some vodka and food and himself went home. Nastya was already waiting. She was sitting and chewing on the corner of her scarf. Heavyset, a nuisance, but not bad looking. She had a figure. Pekalov, who himself was still young, considered that after a couple of drinks the figure is all that counts.

"Oh, you're my beautiful babe!" Pekalov started gushing in rapture. The vodka and food had been brought, no one was bothering them, and his anticipation was keen. "My beautiful babe! You'll forget me as soon as my money melts away, won't you?" He laughed. "But it won't all be gone tomorrow. Just look!" He drew out a stack of bills and shook them as if bragging.

She was silent, still chewing on her scarf. She was a shy woman. But obviously she understood that things were going downhill and that after he had squandered all his money, she would be all he had left. "Nastya, the soldier's wife," he said and kissed her. But she just sat there shyly until he started forcibly undressing her. "How good we've got it, how great!" he kept muttering. "Can it be possible that in the future people won't understand all this good that's inside us . . . "

It was dusk when he started getting ready, sent Nastya home, and hurriedly left the house. With a tipsy gait he made his way in the dark, guided around the place by drunken memory. Once he got in the vicinity of the town he picked up his pace. He almost ran. Only when he came out to the river did he realize that it was nighttime and naturally no one would be digging at that hour, so why was he rushing? "Oh, yeah, just to check!"

Stamping in his boots across the pebbles on the river

embankment, he pushed the brush aside and was near the mouth of the tunnel when he almost stumbled on Yaryga.

"Well? They didn't run off?"

"No. They're sleeping over there under the scrub oak."

"Thank God!"

Pekalov climbed up a little knoll, sat down on a rock, and, relaxing after his rush to get back, had a smoke.

Yaryga stood nearby and looked out at the river.

"I keep thinking—won't we be drowned tomorrow? If not tomorrow, then the day after?"

"Here we go again!" Pekalov said. "Tell me why God would tear the river apart just to drown fools like you and me. Why, so to say, spoil the heart of things?"

"That's true," Yaryga agreed.

Then they sat together. Yaryga wrapped himself in his old torn sheepskin coat and fell asleep on the spot. Pekalov was on a drunken high and didn't take his eyes off the path of moonlight on the river. They say it's a place mermaids inhabit. If only he could touch one! He had another smoke while admiring the river, then climbed into the tunnel. He dropped and relighted the candle several times. Finally he got to the end of the site, the earthen wall where the last dig forward had stopped. He went up close. Drip, drip, drip. It fell on his outstretched hand. It was trickling. Oh, you damn river, damn little river.

The next day things got downright scary. No joke. Digging ahead five more feet, but going deeper, the men again let out a shout, "It's dripping!" Other voices yelled in answer, "Over here, too!" It was if a spell had been put on them. In one place where they dug through it was dripping only slightly, but in a new spot it was an outright trickle, like rain from a roof, with drops pattering down in a steady stream and glistening in the candlelight. Pekalov dashed over to one of the men. As he kept digging ahead, little streams of water ran down his bare back.

"Never mind, brothers, we'll plow through this. The ground'll be hard again up ahead," Pekalov tried to reassure them.

The man who had streams running down his back put aside his pick, wiped the sweat off his face, and asked, "You think it's hard up above?"

"How's that?"

"I mean, at least on top, maybe there's a hard layer holding?" He poked his fist into the arch overhead. Without the least effort he stuck his arm into soft mud almost up to the elbow, and when he drew his fist out, a rush of water spurted down, as if several leaky buckets had finally collapsed, all at once. The noise of the spill frightened the digging crew; pushing and shoving they all rushed to the exit. They even ran, bumping against others who had fallen down, clambering over shovels and picks, trampling on the lighted candles and putting them out, then rushing on in total darkness.

They huddled together down at the exit, where Pekalov, who had caught up, tried to calm them down. He got the vodka jug and set it out. "I'll pour you some, I'll pour it right now.

"Brothers, brothers!" he called out to them, but it didn't help.

"We'll get vodka some other place!" some yelled as they headed off, but Pekalov managed to hold back at least a few, who were hesitating for the moment.

"Now come on! I'm gonna get back in there myself right now! I'll show you!" He lighted a candle with a trembling hand and went climbing into the tunnel. He had to go. And the men waited at the entrance.

Yaryga caught up with him. Sheltering the candle and with tears in his voice, Pekalov swore at him. "Why did you leave them? They'll take off."

"They won't leave. I've already opened the jug for them and put out some grub. They won't go anywhere till they've gorged themselves."

"But it's scary, Yaryga . . . "

They went over to the place where the water had gushed out: it was running in a stream, but weaker than before. When the one digger had punched a hole through the overhead layer with his fist, he apparently hit a pocket of water, and now it was pouring out. The water trickled on while Pekalov and Yaryga talked. Pekalov held the candle close to the hole, Yaryga cupped his hands, and in an instant his huge hands had filled with water.

"It's awful," Pekalov said. "But maybe we can patch it up somehow?"

Yaryga nodded: even that big drunk Alyoshka had always said that the earth in the tunnel could be supported by an iron roof, even that they could run a pipe in to take the water off.

"Let's try it," Pekalov agreed. "Course it won't hold the river back, but at least it won't scare everybody so."

"Exactly."

Pekalov hung the candle up by sticking the sharp hook of the candlestick into a side arch and grabbed a pick. "Yaryga, let's dig through a bit to get this stream behind us." Yaryga got another pick. Pekalov dug on the right and Yaryga on the left. In half an hour they changed places, then dug their way ahead at a slower pace. They were careful, and it was better that they, rather than the drunken gang, dig through this dangerous area. Especially with their nerves frayed, the men could make a serious blunder. By the time Pekalov and Yaryga got a full foot ahead, they both were wet from head to toe. But then, farther on, there was no dripping. Feeling a bit braver, they began widening the tunnel when, suddenly, footsteps were heard from behind. Every one of the habitual little drunks had come down into the tunnel; maybe they thought they would take a look at the drowning victims, at the two dead men. Yaryga and Pekalov were calmly pounding away with their picks, and they kept on working without looking around. In the meantime, the men compared the curtain of dripping water with the fact that up ahead everything was dry and normal.

"Take over for us," Yaryga said to them.

They didn't answer. Then one said in an agreeable tone, "Uh-huh."

Before starting to make their way out, Pekalov and Yaryga gave them strict instructions not to chip the upper layer as they worked, but even to tap the clay in with their shovels as they moved along. "That clay's holding some water pockets—it's not the river, it's just water. The river's a lot higher overhead."

Up on the hill Pekalov and Yaryga opened the jug and took a drink and chewed on some bread.

Pekalov gave Yaryga some money and sent him to buy a little sheet metal and a few wood slabs and boards. He wanted to send someone else, not Yaryga, but there was the risk that one of the others would take the money and run away. Every man counted now. When the water had gushed out, five of them took off.

"Hookay," Yaryga said, as if thinking aloud. "Turns out the worst of the bunch stayed on—the ones that either the Cossacks, the penal camp, or the noose are just itching to get."

"Maybe they're pining for you, too—but you're going to town."

Yaryga didn't answer; he just grinned.

The morning after the usual drinking spree, they started assembling support pillars in the tunnel; this was as much for peace of mind as it was for strengthening the roof of the tunnel. Yaryga and Timka hewed out the props, the others bolstered them in place and covered them in metal sheeting. The mood at work now was livelier. They placed props not just at the points of maximum danger, but also in the side arches.

At the break they even sang a little—they hadn't sung for a long time. While rounding off one of the pillars, Yaryga beckoned Pekalov over, and above the din of the drunken song, he whispered that he finally had found out who the killer was, "the one who disposed of those two men of ours."

"It was Lychov," he went on. "He's the one, the bastard. I saw him just now sharpening the reverse end of his crowbar. He'll swing it back—and that'll be the end of the man behind him."

"You think he's settling scores?" Pekalov whispered, picking out Lychov from the bunch sprawled out on the grass.

Yaryga grinned. "Scores? Naw, he just likes doing it." Both of them grew thoughtful. How to act and what to do so that nobody went down to dig alone with Lychov?

Sure enough, after his drink Lychov, eyes rolling, dirty and bare to the waist, was the first to get up from the grass and shout, "Well, who's going with me? Let's go!" Then Yaryga, slowly but not lingering and without a word, followed him off. He just winked to Pekalov, as if to say, keep the others back, tipple a little more with them. To delay them was the simplest thing in the world, nobody was in a hurry to go back in the tunnel, or the hole, as they called it. They drank and hollered. Timka and his workmate even dozed off after downing their booze.

An hour later Yaryga appeared and said loudly, "Lychov, the bastard, evidently ran off! He's nowhere to be found."

"Oh, yeah?"

They rushed around here and there, yelling and calling, but no answer. One of the men angrily cursed him. "He was awful desperate," Yaryga said, with a wave of the hand. "I thought he'd be digging longer than any of us."

"Yeah, that's what we thought!" others said.

When they went down into the tunnel, Yaryga and Pekalov shoveled first, and Yaryga told him, "Here," and pointed to a side arch.

"Won't he stink?"

"Shouldn't. I put him down at least three feet. Like in a tomb. With a board on top."

"So, Yaryga, you've got lots of blood on your hands, right?"

"You call this blood?"

When the work shift changed they squeezed themselves through the passage and took up the picks at the end. Yaryga dug on briskly, even cheerfully. Digging and trenching had become unexpectedly easy—they had hit soft rock.

The soft rock kept going, it was easier to dig, but then they got into detritus, and the very looks of the light gravel mixed with pebbles was cause for new fear. It seemed as if the river bottom was showing through, baring itself, and that any minute all this would collapse and tons of river water would surge down in such a flood that not only would it be impossible to escape, but even to stand. The weight itself would kill them. Every day earth slides occurred: the ground shook softly and crashed down. They had used up all the supplies for roof supports. Pekalov kept reassuring them—"We'll buy more, for sure"—until Yaryga shut him up.

"Quit lying. I know there's no money left."

There could have been enough money, but after one of the quiet earth slides, Burov left and with him one of the hopeless boozers, one with scars on his head and a bare scalp. They sneaked away during the night. They broke into the little store chest, took an uncorked jug but nothing more, apparently afraid of instigating an angry chase. But besides the jug, they fished the bundle of money out from under Pekalov's head as he slept and made off with it. Only four of them were left now in the hole, counting Timka, who was closer and closer to snapping from the vodka. They worked in pairs: one dug, the other rested. Then all four shoveled, stretching and tossing the dirt over to each other. Pekalov totally lost heart. He lay down on the little hill and in a trance looked to the other side, where the swamp was.

"I'm young. A bungler," he said, blinking back tears.

"That's it exactly—you're young," Yaryga laughed.

Then and there Yaryga starting gathering up his things. "I'm leaving, too."

"No!" Pekalov screamed. He damned everybody and everything. He lay and beat the ground with his fist and cursed Yaryga. "I shouldn't have spent the money to put in the props. You shouldn't have killed Lychov—because of that, Burov and his pal ran away."

Yaryga laughed. "You fool, they ran away because of the earth slides." If he, Yaryga, dreamed about the earth caving in, what was there to say about the others?

"I didn't have any dreams like that!" Pekalov shouted scornfully, to which Yaryga just repeated, "That's it exactly—you're young."

Yaryga would've left, but he wanted to have a smoke before setting out and he was taking his time. Just then Kutyr, covered with dirt, jumped out of the tunnel and waving his shaky, dirty arms shouted, "We passed halfway! We've gone under half the river!

"Half the river!" he yelled. "Half the river!"

"How do you know?"

Still shouting at the top of his lungs Kutyr said that he had just measured it—two hundred yards! Once Alyoshka also had rowed out on the river and stretched a rope from the bank to his boat and with his keen eye had calculated the point where both banks of the river were equidistant, then afterward they had measured how many yards were on the rope. It was two hundred—that's half the river! Once the idea had struck home, Pekalov also started yelling. His face grew pale and he trembled all over.

"Hey, boys! Time to celebrate! Let's drink to it—we're halfway there!"

Pekalov rushed around, opened the chest, ran up to the tunnel entrance and bellowed out, "Hey in there, m'boys! That's enough—let's drink!" But only Timka was there. He clambered out and naturally headed straight for the vodka, but Pekalov kept calling into the hole of the tunnel. "Hey, hey, boys!" he went on yelling, until Yaryga came up and grabbed him by the shoulder.

"Are you cracking or what? There are only four of us, or have you lost count?" He pulled him aside, but his young boss still went on jumping and screaming.

"Hey, boys!" he kept on. "The vodka's all yours now! I'm not gonna lock it up! Boys!" Tearing both the latch and the recently repaired lock itself off the chest with a crowbar, he swung and threw them both into the river, where they sank with a splash.

That evening Pekalov rushed off to town. "Some money. I'll get some money!" He shook at the thought that there wasn't enough money now.

It was dark inside the house; the rich peasant Salkov hadn't settled any of his family here yet, however he had put new locks on. Pekalov knew a window that could be opened from the outside, and he crawled in, feeling his way in the dark. Nothing had been said in the sale agreement about clothing, so Pekalov gathered his more decent things into a bundle and took it, together with a box of personal items and his good rifle. Keyed up and hurrying from house to house, he sold everything quickly. Never mind that it was after dark—at least nobody would see how dirty he was. Anyway, people didn't look him in the eye, but just gave him the price he asked, as if buying stolen goods.

In the dark under Nastya's windows he gave a whistle, but when her mother looked out, he hid behind a tree to keep from showing her how threadbare and dirty he was. He was breathing heavily. Then Nastya came out.

"Gee, look at you!" she said and grew silent, nibbling on the end of her scarf.

He asked her to come down to the river, and explained, "I don't have my house anymore."

"I know."

She walked with him a short way in the darkness. They

were almost at the river when she said, "We've gotta part. I can't take any more shame on myself. I've gotta live my life, gotta wait for my husband to come back from the army . . . " He wanted to caress Nastya, at least give her a hug, but even in the dark his hands looked filthy, and his clothes alone would get her dirty, because she was all fresh and clean in her pretty gray scarf. Holding her arms back, she herself stuck out her lips and kissed him. "Good-bye, sweet. We've sure loved each other, but now, see, it's time."

Then she flew away, a clean little gray sparrow . . . He kept crumpling the money. Should he give a last present or not? And he didn't give it. He didn't have a kopeck to spare. He stood alone in the darkness, dejected, feeling stingy for the first time in his life.

Digging smoothly ahead, the four men took turns, working in pairs, and they had already gone about fifteen yards beyond the halfway point when suddenly something happened to Timka. Pekalov and Yaryga were shoveling, when from the depths of the hole Kutyr yelled for them to come. They hurried down, squeezed into the pit, and in the flickering candlelight saw Timka sitting with his neck craned and looking up. Suddenly he ran his hand across the overhang of earth just above him. He touched the top arch and muttered, "The ole river's ringing . . . Ya hear it?" He stroked it again. They listened carefully. Nothing was ringing, of course.

They told Timka to go out and take a break, but he kept repeating that the water was ringing, that the river was ringing, so then they led him out of the tunnel. He sat down on the sand. The vodka was stored just a little ways off, and an hour later when they had shoveled out the dirt they had dug and came out to rest, it turned out that Timka had finished the whole jug. He had quietly gone off his rocker, without a single shout. He didn't even really drink the vodka—more than half a gallon had been left—he just poured it into his mouth and let it trickle out. He went on splashing the vodka in, but it streamed out along his throat onto his chest and knees. "What're you wasting our supply for?" Yaryga still from a distance shouted angrily, but Timka just poured it on down and smiled. When they took the jug away from him, he took a handful of dirt and sifted it from one hand to another. He was playing in the sand like a little kid. "The ole river," he kept saying, "little ole river . . . it's a-singin'!" The other three all stood there, listening in silence to the rustle of the sand as he sifted it back and forth.

"He'll come out of it," Yaryga said.

"He overdid the vodka," Kutyr added. "He'll recover."

But he didn't recover; when they sat down to eat, he got on his feet, but it seemed that it was hard for him to stand. He was standing behind a bush, but when they looked around again, Timka was already in the middle of the river. He was swimming to the other side, then he sank. The cold whirlpools that for so many years hadn't allowed people or even boats to pass had already grabbed Timka. "Ole river," he yelled with a choke. "Lit-tle ole riv-er!" Yaryga dived into the river, but even by swimming fast as he could, he couldn't get there in time. Timka had gone to the bottom. Yaryga didn't even find his body. He looked, but he lost courage when he got close to the cold whirlpools. He whipped around and headed back. He was swimming slowly, taking his time. Peering closely, Pekalov and Kutyr couldn't understand why his face was blue and twisted. Only when Yaryga was first some ten yards from shore, then about five, in shallow water, did they understand that he couldn't stand up. He just struggled, somehow crawled out on a sandbar, and tried to pull himself up, but he couldn't stand. Pekalov and Kutyr grabbed hold of him, dragged him out, and laid him down on dry sand. Yaryga lay there for a long time, then he rose and cautiously made his way to the chest, but he didn't take a drink. He poured a little vodka into his hand and rubbed it along his spine. Kutyr and Pekalov went over, turned him on his stomach, and took turns at rubbing his back until it was all red.

He had barely recovered his breath when he took off.

Pekalov hung on to him. "But wait! Who in hell acts like this!" Pekalov couldn't believe that everything was simply over. He ran after him, begged and pleaded, but when Pekalov grabbed him by the arms, Yaryga shoved him away and, taking a short swing, punched him between the eyes. By the time Pekalov could see clearly again, Yaryga was long gone.

The only one left with Pekalov was Kutyr, an old, broken-down thief who wasn't able or capable of stealing anymore because his hands shook so from drinking and fighting. He wasn't going anywhere. It was evening. Pekalov wept; it was a blow. Trying to console him, Kutyr stretched a shaky arm forward and pointed. "Take a look over there."

"What is it?"

"We're up to there now, see?" Kutyr pointed to a certain point out on the river—the spot they had reached underground. It was a distant point, undiscernible on the water as wave toppled upon wave.

Now they dug by turns, saving their strength by reducing the width. The tunnel became narrow—a burrow was all it really was. First Pekalov would dig and Kutyr would shovel, then they'd trade off. At one place suddenly there was a cave-in from above, but they paid no attention. They were used to it.

There was a hullabaloo under way in the middle of the road. Three blind men were thrashing a little boy who had led them into some kind of trouble.

"Ow, ouch!" the little boy screamed. "Ow, I didn't do it on purpose!"

Dust swirled over the road as if a troika had just passed. With the blind men stamping their feet and waving their arms in the middle of a road, it was hard to know how to get through. Pekalov, covered with dirt and clothes in tatters, went around them and slipped into the tavern.

"I'll be sitting in the far corner," Pekalov said immediately to the waiter so that he would let him in, which he did.

There weren't many people. Pekalov craved something hot, but didn't permit himself the cabbage stew (he was holding on to what little money there was left); instead he drank glass after glass of tea. Shaking and feverish—a shabby fellow with sunken cheeks—he sat there without a thought in his head.

"The rains'll be starting soon," the waiter observed as he brought him another glass of tea from the samovar. He tried to start at least some kind of conversation about the weather. Pekalov added, "Yeah, the rains . . . " He feared for himself. Wet weather could create underground pockets of water, could cause something unforeseen with the river.

When Pekalov left the tavern, the blind men were still beating the little boy. They flogged him and twisted his ears while he screamed. Finally managing to break away, the youngster jumped to the side.

"Now make it by yourselves, bleary-eyes!" the boy screamed from a distance as he ran farther and father away. The blind men were angry and they yelled, too, and swore to God that they would never forgive their guide for his stupidity and malice.

"Hey, good fathers!" Pekalov called to them, and since the blind men were obviously hungry and wandering like lost souls, Pekalov promised them some nourishment, even a little vodka, and some ordinary work—digging underground. The blind men listened attentively.

"Is this God's work?" asked the elder one, who was way past forty.

Pekalov answered that yes, it was God's work. Not thievery. Not some other abomination. He just didn't say that he was digging a tunnel under the river. It seemed to him that at that bitter moment when he was left alone with Kutyr,

God had bid him to be silent. Why should they know that the river was right overhead? Let them dig without fear . . . There were three of the blind men, and just as soon as they agreed, Pekalov hurried them off.

"Let's be on our way, dear souls, let's move right on!"

"What's the rush?"

"Oh, the rain's gonna start!" Pekalov fussed about. He was afraid the little guide would come back to them and, repentant, he would spoil everything.

Pekalov dug for three weeks with the blind men, who, since they were unable to see, feared nothing. After about every thirty feet they dug, they would stop work, get on their knees, and pray fervently.

"Dear Lord, have mercy on us!"

Another thirty feet, then, "Mercy upon us."

And again, "Lord, have mercy!"

They passed through the crumbling sediment, they overcame a frightening layer of pebbles that kept tinkling down, after that—clay, then sediment again, and finally they dug out to a huge boulder beyond which stood the untrampled brush of the swampy shore. They climbed out to the surface. In the old legend of the Urals it surprised everyone that blind men were better and more reliable than others in finishing the job.

One version of the story of the tunnel under the Ural ends with Pekalov's father and prosperous brother taking him away into seclusion so he wouldn't do harm to the family name. It seems they hid him for good in a shack somewhere under the watchful eye of an old woman—a form of exile. Or maybe a form of healing. It was there that he ended his days. Sometimes he emerged, gazed around (during a storm the wind brought moisture), and peered out at the horizon. "Is it far to the Ural?" He was totally alone.

At the very end of this long story Pekalov became a saint and even rose to heaven, God knows what for—maybe for audacity. (In our current parlance, "for his drive to succeed.") On the other side of the river he neither discovered a spring nor built a church. Besides, Pekalov himself was completely human, a sinner, and it's only in the epilogue of the legend that you find passages that try, as many final words do, to create the image of a saint. You never know—maybe it'll take hold.

The blind are people who cope with their loss, so it's said. In those days blind men would take a boy, usually an orphan at an early age, feed and clothe him, in exchange for which he then would lead them through God's wide world. The blind men weren't the kindest people. They mistreated the boy, so that unconsciously day by day resentment built up in him. At the same time he was growing; he began to form a sense of things in the world; he got into mischief, and from time to time he took revenge, a very special and even unique kind. After a long trek on the road the blind men needed to relieve themselves.

"Dear boy," they would say to him, "now, well, lad, find us some secluded spot to go." And he would lead them to the walls of a nunnery or a monastery, right below the windows. In either case, the spot would be such that they wouldn't suspect any mischief. It was truly quiet and secluded, not by a street or a market, and it's not hard at all to imagine the scene when the blind men would be squatting, then from the window someone notices the blasphemy in progress, there's shouting and running and they get beaten with sticks. But naturally the little boy, all doubled over with laughter, was secretly peeking out at it all from a distance, so that after the blind men were beaten by keen-sighted ones, he would stand before them again and explain that the sheltered quiet of the place had lured him there, and that all this was a mishap, that he himself, God as his witness, had been squatting there alongside them.

There's a bridge over the Ural now at that spot, and until

quite recently a chapel stood nearby. On the left side of the entrance shone a drawing of an ascension, half-obliterated from worshipers rubbing it: Pekalov, with a halo around his head, being carried to heaven by two angels. Old women who came with their baskets from the market often sat in the shade of the chapel. Time passed. Then one spring the chapel collapsed, the drawing disappeared, and nothing remained there as a reminder of the madman who dug a tunnel and lodged himself in peoples' memory and, say what you may, became a legend.

2

One of the originators of acupuncture, a Chinese physician who, it's said, lived in the seventh century, by force of his talent reached exceptional heights in the history of healing, but he did not become a legend. He became famous and powerful, but not a legend.

From the beginning he never stopped and was determined, as we would say, to take his career to the very top. Finally his genius achieved full recognition in the eyes of his contemporaries. He began to heal not mere warriors, but generals, and then soon the emperor himself. He became a great court physician, maybe the very greatest, with all sorts of honors. His name entered the history books, but not legend.

Legends sprang up only after he performed one particular experiment—a final and, in fact, absurd one. The great healer had treated the emperor dozens of times, as well as members of the royal family, but one time when the emperor, who was already aging, complained of a headache and the usual popular remedies didn't help, the physician proposed cutting open his head. No doubt this would have killed the emperor, but essentially he wanted to perform what is now called a lobotomy. Possibly the zealous healer no longer wanted to cure his patient, but rather out of thirst for knowledge just wanted to see with his own eyes what was inside the head—how it looked. What is this puzzling pain and why doesn't it abate? The emperor, old but retaining his common sense, declined. He figured that after all one can live for years with a headache, but the skull is not a purse to be opened and closed at will. The physician insisted. Then the emperor emphatically refused and began to shout as only a Chinese emperor can. During the night the healer stole into the royal chambers and tried to cut open the sleeping emperor's head. Accused of attempted assassination, he was executed the next day.

A legend doesn't have to be shouted hoarsely to make itself heard in its own age—and on to the next century and farther. A legend shouts through the beauty of its story. It's as if absurdity and the clear recognition of its appeal overwhelm common sense and cause it to be buried and forgotten.

In the past men and women grieved that they would be forgotten, would be eaten by worms, and no trace would remain of them and their deeds, and in our day they wail about losing their roots and their ties to their ancestors. But isn't this one and the same? Isn't it the extension in time of joint human spiritual pain?

According to legend, the trader Pekalov, a man of vulgar tastes and easy morals, stupidly embarked on a certain project, the project failed, and he himself remained the same man of questionable character as before. But as it turns out, the very duration of his persistence constitutes its own charm and mystery. For, as he takes up his cause again a second and third time, the demonstration of an elemental human persistence suggests a man of quite different character. Even as he was called mad and obsessed, other words were used to place him in high esteem, and if, hungry and in tatters, he achieves his goal and dies tragically, it is inevitable that the word "hero" be used, though cautiously so, in making the ultimate assessment.

If people around him can't understand his goal, if the

obvious illogic of his quest is something almost saintly, then it's just a short step to the word "holy" or to some use of the word—just in case—in more modest form. For instance, in the form of going to heaven on the wings of angels. He went to heaven, it's said, and in time we'll decide whether he was a saint or not. That's what the legend did.

"Well, so finally we've met again . . . ," my old friend from childhood said gloomily. He was already balding.

I nodded, "Yes, now we've met."

We had taken a long time to agree where to meet after so many years, had twisted words this way and that, and suddenly both agreed easily and immediately: we didn't meet either at my house or his, but at a little restaurant table around which there scurried a waiter who was unhappy with us. "Not at my house and not at his" had its own logic. Neither wanted to see exactly where and how well the other was living, didn't want to know *how's life* and *how's it going* (this is your wife and these are the kids, and this is your apartment, so forth and so on); we didn't want to see the present objects, the present routine, and in general the present time. My childhood friend didn't want a drink. He started the conversation by explaining that now he drinks only mineral water, stomach problems not permitting even the best, most refined vodka. I'm also on the wagon, also drink only mineral water, also have my reasons. He doesn't drink even coffee and has high blood pressure. Me, too, no coffee. He doesn't eat anything spicy. I do, but a diet is also in the offing. Now everything is in the offing.

Neither of us complains, although essentially for us and our memories nothing could have been gloomier than an encounter like this. We're finished products. We satisfied the desires of our youth and fulfilled primary needs, even propagated the species—we've got children and even grandchildren. In its turn, self-awareness developed to such a relatively high degree as to show life from a bird's-eye view and that's when, at least abstractly, we can reconcile ourselves to the fact that everyone is mortal, including us. That's the way it was. Neither of us complained, but while we met, a sense of chill came over us. We felt cold and realized that it wouldn't be bad to dig down deeply (as he put it, *deep into the layers of the pie of time*) where there's lots of sunshine and where, with each layer, things get warmer and warmer, because childhood is closer.

A topic worthy of the imagination of drinkers of mineral water even emerged. Our ancestors came from different and varied backgrounds and places, and, displaying even considerable animation, we compared and checked the presence in each other of an ability that every talkative person has—to take a guess at the question of just what constitutes the benefits and shortcomings of having ties that bind people together.

The grumbling waiter had stopped grumbling and heads were no longer turning in our direction when, now relaxed, we stared with fascination at the slowly rising bubbles in the mineral water. We ordered two more bottles with such bubbles. Might as well drink more. Then my childhood friend said a word that sounded as if I were hearing it for the first time.

"The loss . . ."

"What?" I thought I hadn't quite heard.

3

Typically enough, Pekalov deceived the blind men in his reply to their question. "If this is doing God's work, why is there no point to it?" they asked, after Pekalov had set them to digging without telling them anything, not even about the river overhead. He answered them without hesitation, dissembling, so it seemed, as he tried to put their doubts to rest, but essentially also working on the legend and its creators. "Who says God's work has a point? That's just it: man's work has a point. For that reason God causes us to think that there's no point in this, but you feel like doing it and it has to be done." Adhering to model naïveté, the legend makes the case even stronger: "If the reason for the job is clear and logical, why should it be inspired from above?"

Pekalov brought the three blind men into his tunnel ("This way, poor men, this way!"), and in the darkness they stumbled on the shovels and hit their heads and shoulders on the low archway, but they weren't aware of the darkness around them. They just heard the sputtering of the candles. Pretty soon they got accustomed to the place. At first they shoveled out the dirt, but then they took to digging, relieving Pekalov and Kutyr. The third and youngest of them turned out to be especially easygoing and nice, according to the legend. He was quiet and occasionally would sing prayers as he worked. "O Lord, have mercy on me-ee," he drawled out softly.

And when Kutyr drank down his vodka and moistened his injured hand with the few drops left in the glass, he asked them, "So, my poor men, will ya have a touch?" The blind men refused. They ate lightly and even vodka didn't tempt them. At this point it became clear that as workmen they were ideal—they were cheap. Working in shifts finally became genuine routine; since the blind men were without a guide, they never moved a foot away from the site. They set up a makeshift but sturdy shelter amid the brush right near the mouth of the tunnel, and Pekalov and Kutyr slept there, too. There was no confusion and no need at all for calling them out to work. It had to be said that providence had sent the blind men at a fatal moment.

However, one concern developed: the blind men lost their directions. Not knowing that a river was above them and the danger it meant, they unwittingly dug farther and farther upward, and to all entreaties to keep to the trajectory already taken, they answered that they themselves knew how to dig, because now the Virgin Mary was guiding them.

Why exactly the Virgin was guiding them neither Pekalov nor Kutyr understood. Pekalov tried to persuade, cajole, and entice them in any way he could, but the blind men went on doing as they pleased, and from time to time, as they grew more confident at the job, they might suddenly swing to the left or hit steeply upward. Support pillars had long since been abandoned. Once when Pekalov and Kutyr returned from a break and took their places, they froze in fear. The blind man who sang prayers was slaving away and then suddenly plunged his pick into the earth overhead with such tremendous force that water instantly gushed out. The water surged so powerfully that it was impossible to escape—in any case the water would overcome them. And Pekalov didn't run. Kutyr did, but there was no way he could run the whole 250 feet of the tunnel in time. Water was almost up to their knees. In bewilderment the blind man shouted, "What's happening?" but went on digging without stop. The water poured into their boots and kept rising. Now Pekalov, too, was essentially blind. The two candles that had stood on the ground were washed away immediately.

The blind man, who knew nothing about the river, shouted to Pekalov, "Let's take a smoke. This groundwater will subside soon," and asked Pekalov to roll and light him a cigarette. But he had to shout to Pekalov a second time. Coming to himself, Pekalov mechanically fumbled through his pockets and only then noticed that they were dry and that the water hadn't gone any higher, or that it was rising very slowly, and that also meant that they were—saved! Pekalov himself lighted the roll of tobacco and handed it to the blind man. The water stood a bit, then started sinking, sucked away somewhere below, and the blind man grumbled, "Hey, you got so shook up that you rolled it bad. Even I could've done a better job." He finished smoking and took up his pick again. Kutyr came back. He also thought it was groundwater, and now he impatiently pounded on the big rocks and increased the outward drain. He kept pounding, searching for a hole—and found it. With a hollow rumble the water swept down below, leaving underfoot only mud and slush. Pekalov, shaken, left to get a drink of vodka. He clambered out of the hole, stepped over to a grassy spot, and dropped down. He just wanted to lie in the warm sunshine. Not far away the two other blind men— one old, the other young—were sleeping during their break.

The little boy who had been the guide turned up at the first fall rains. He had quenched his wanderlust, completely satisfied his yearning for pranks, and now that summer had ended was looking for a steady supply of food. But the blind men didn't want to go on a long trek until they had finished this God's work.

"Kind sirs, let's be on our way," the boy urged them, now swearing that he would lead them by the best and easiest roads.

Pekalov, leaning his head outside the shelter, listened to the conversation with alarm. But the little guide didn't guess at trying to scare the blind men with the danger of the river and a cave-in; he was too preoccupied with his own fate. Pekalov relaxed and again took cover in the shelter as rain lashed the riverbank almost in a downpour.

Both blind men, the old one and the young one, standing near the shelter, refused to give in to the boy, even out of pity.

"Be on your way. God will feed you!" the old one shouted out sternly. He still couldn't forgive him for that dirty trick at the monastery.

"Kind sirs, I confess," the little boy began to whimper, maybe even genuinely.

The rain poured, the old blind man stood motionless, rain streamed off his bald head and splashed onto his back and shoulders. The young blind man stood nearby, his blond hair as long as a girl's dangling in wet strands.

"On your way."

The boy left, and they both stood still until, through the rain, they heard him stepping through the brush.

The blind men worked like a newly charged machine, but when detritus and large stones again appeared, they got nervous. As if by mutual consent they prayed less often and kept trying to dig upward. They became uncontrollable, and Pekalov sometimes threatened to send them away and sometimes asked them kindly and humbly not to dig that way. Kutyr almost snatched the pick away from them and yelled, "Why the hell are you digging upward? Stupid blind fools!" After that they almost came to blows. It was frightening how crumbly the earth had become. It was no longer the clay that held harmless water pockets. That same day the old blind man saw the Virgin in the tunnel, closer up than ever before. He let out a yell and cried out that he had seen her, that her dear image had shined before his eyes, and she had pointed him in this very direction—that he should dig upward. He had seen her clearly and plainly and he pointed up—there.

"How could you see her? Have you ever even seen her in an icon?" Kutyr, whose hands were shaking more than usual, shouted angrily.

"I saw her. Saw her many times. I was eleven when I went blind," the old man said calmly.

They were already flying at each other when an idea occurred to Pekalov. He headed for the exit, quickly but without running. He took measured steps, and only when he had reached the mouth of the tunnel and had counted his careful steps to four hundred did he turn around and rush back into the depths of the tunnel again. Now he ran, moving as fast as he could, and as soon as he reached the end he shouted, "It's true—dig upward!" and he was out of breath.

Once he caught his breath, he started to explain, but then shaking all over, he started bustling about.

"Come on, my dear men, let's move!" Pekalov grabbed a crowbar, then a shovel, trying to excite the blind men, who were already worked up without him. "I see her, I do!" shouted the old man, flailing furiously into the earth. Right next to him Kutyr, who had guessed what Pekalov had in mind, over and over struck his crowbar upward, and the two of them even hindered each other. They dug like madmen. Very soon Pekalov heard a scraping sound: the two blind men, both with picks, were pounding at a big immobile rock. Sparks flew. Throwing aside their picks, the men grabbed crowbars, and then the sparks started flying fiercely, but, of course, they couldn't see them.

"I see her!" shouted the old blind man. "I do!"

It made no sense to pound on the whole rock, and Pekalov grabbed them by the arms.

"Stop! This is a rock! Are you blind, or what?" he yelled angrily, by now not hearing his very own words.

But they heard them.

"Blind—yourself!" yelled the old man irately.

"Come help me!" Pekalov shouted to Kutyr, and only together, with their fists, did they manage to drive the blind men away from the spot.

The rock turned out to be enormous, and to figure out how to go about moving it required some thinking. They needed to trench around the rock so that by its own force it would fall out, but fall gradually so that the river, if it was still overhead, wouldn't swallow them all up instantly. A boulder would act as a plug, even if it shifted and was no longer a tight fit. With the blind men out of the way Pekalov and Kutyr were able to confer; they inspected the rock as closely and calmly as possible, but they still couldn't locate a corner—the rock was rounded off. "It's a boulder," Pekalov decided, and Kutyr nodded, but then they heard the rustle of cautious steps. All keyed up, the blind men were making their way closer again.

The rock was like an enormous egg lying on its side. And if it was so enormous that it would be impossible to move it aside, then there was no choice but to loosen the ground around it and let it slide down from its own heavy weight. "And what if we open up a hole into the river?" "But what else can we do?" Pekalov and Kutyr discussed the options in whispers, and the blind men stood behind them, also whispering and not moving to leave. They were too agitated, but also they harbored the thought that they were purposely being held back from the sacred vision, that they were being robbed on the spot.

So it turned out that when Pekalov and Kutyr had widened the dig site, the blind men immediately wedged themselves in to shovel. As they worked, gaunt and half-famished, they struck up a chant of psalms. They all dug at once. The oval shape of the rock could finally be seen; the earth under it was soft, almost tender, it seemed. Bending over, Pekalov clawed the earth like a dog. "It's moving! It's moving!" Kutyr yelled to him when he noticed that the rock had shifted slightly, but Pekalov kept clawing the dirt away, and the rock grew rounder and more distinct as it hung over them. There was a scraping sound; they all froze in place. The scraping grew into a ominous sound, as if the earth had let out a thud, and the huge boulder came down upon them. The blind men leaped forward; the candle went out.

Pekalov managed to see that the blind man who had been bustling about between him and Kutyr was crushed flat. He also realized that the rest of them hadn't drowned, that there was no rush of water. But also there was no light—it was pitch dark, although suddenly the air smelled pungent, spicy, and like the riverbank. Then the loose boulder shook and rolled again, crushing Pekalov's arm from the elbow down, and he immediately lost consciousness.

Kutyr leaped aside. Before the candle went out he managed to the see the crushed, spread-out body of the blind man, and nearby Pekalov's contorted figure. But the candle was blown out, and left suddenly in darkness, Kutyr couldn't understand why there was no light and why he couldn't make out anything around him, if there was an opening and if there was the smell of fresh air. He was seized with fear. He scrambled in the dark to get to the men who had been pinned down.

"Powers of heaven and powers of earth . . . ," the old thief muttered, his teeth chattering in fright.

Only when he had managed to drag Pekalov out of the tunnel did Kutyr realize why there was no light at the end of the tunnel: it was nighttime.

Naturally the darkness didn't frighten the blind men, and they dashed ahead. Moreover, when they didn't hear the voice of the one who had been hit by the boulder, they decided that their companion was already far ahead and they headed for the way out through the opening. They found it quickly. There on the other side of the river, in the brush and swamp pits, they cried out in anguish and called to the Holy Virgin, who for some reason now had abandoned them and didn't hear their cries. At night on this bank no one at all saw or heard them. The village slept. They floundered about, up to their waists in the swamp, and no longer called out to the Virgin.

"Help, people!" they called. "Help!" Then, sensing their misfortune and ruin, they called to their guide, shouting that they would forgive him for everything. "Boy! Lit-tle bo-oy!" They called for him in tender, effeminate-sounding voices.

By morning they were gone. Stumbling around the swamp—a total marsh—grasping at the branches of bushes, they little by little got separated from each other and drowned, bringing an end to their tortures.

The village healer took Pekalov's arm off just below the elbow; the stump dried, but the bandages were kept on. Pekalov woke up in a little house, a shack near a church where a malachite craftsman who had drunk himself to ruin also now lived on charity, a man at one time well known and not poor. A devout old woman cleaned and looked after the place. Pekalov was obviously still a little delirious, because when he woke up he started telling the old woman how soft his lost hand had been—he said this while looking at the stump—and how skillfully the hand held a candle, and how well he remembered that there had been a mole between the third and fourth fingers and where was it now?

Without answering him, the old woman snapped, "Just be quiet!" Then added, "If you go on *raving* I'll send you on your way and you can live as a beggar."

The old woman brought chicken broth for him to drink during the night, and Pekalov drank it, but he was thinking all the time about the tunnel. Can you walk through it? And what if the earth collapsed and the tunnel isn't there anymore? He was worried. He mustn't say even a word about the tunnel. He knew that he should neither remember it nor think about it, that the old woman would keep her word, and maybe would kick him out, like a dog, but the desire to check on the tunnel grew stronger and stronger. Fear and caution created in him a childish wish to go there on the sly—at night, take a quick look around and come back unnoticed. He hid some matches. Catching himself with a groan, he tried lighting a candle with one hand, striking the match on his belt—it worked! This was important, now he could wait until dark, when the old woman would leave. He waited, staring at the blue shadows of twilight on the windows until he fell asleep and dreamed that he was walking through the tunnel.

Waking to the soft patter of rain, he realized that he had overslept and now would have to hurry if he wanted to return unnoticed. He quietly left the house, and throwing a gunnysack over his head, he walked quickly through the rain. Even before reaching the familiar place, he tossed the sack aside and darted into the tunnel. He had come to know the place thoroughly, to know a place any better was impossible, and he let out a laugh, like a child who has found a favorite toy.

Now it wasn't a dream—now he was awake and walking there, and how everything had changed inside! The fall rains had washed all sorts of rubbish into the tunnel, there was a smell of rotting garbage, and besides the litter left after the digging, an abundance of refuse floated on top. Pekalov walked in water up to his knees. Afraid that the water might reach even higher, as he held the candle it occurred to him to take a few matches from his pants pocket and slip them under his collar (in order to do this with only one hand, he had to blow out the candle and light it again).

But the water got lower and lower, then completely disappeared; however, after that he tripped on some mounds of dirt, fell, and dropped his candle. The tunnel grew narrow. Here they had worked when few of the men were left, digging without caring about the width, so that fresh dirt slides had now made the opening impossibly narrow. Getting on his knees he raked dirt away and cleared the passage again. He often hit his head against the arch. The candle went out. He clambered on his knees and even crawled, grabbing onto ledges with his hand and dragging his body forward like a worm. At the end of the way he smelled the pervasive stench of rotting flesh; judging by the distance he had walked and crawled, somewhere nearby the body of the blind man who had been crushed by the boulder lay decomposing. This meant that the boulder itself was nearby. When Pekalov's shoulder bumped against the boulder, a mass of damp earth and clay dropped down with a rustle and covered him. He shook himself and crawled out like a worm from a lump of earth, and after that he saw a soft gray glimmer of light.

When Pekalov came out to the surface he covered his eyes with the palm of his hand. It was like a blow: he had walked out straight into the sunrise.

He had hardly stepped into the swamp when he was seized by an enormous happiness, like a child's. Sunlight poured down on the sedge and the brush and the river, and he jumped from hummock to hummock, forgetting that he hadn't wanted to be seen. "Hey, hey! Yoo-hoo!" he yelled, stretching his arms out to people on the other side, as if sharing his joy with them. The early risers on their way out of the village—some on their way to market, others on some important errand—didn't hear him, but heard the birds. Alarmed by the man and his shouts, the birds soared up with a shrill clamor and circled over the river: it was impossible for the people not to notice them, and then they also noticed the tiny figure of a man who was running and leaping from hummock to hummock and shouting and stretching his arms toward them. The village people all recognized Pekalov. He yelled and waved and twirled the stump of his arm, the palm of his one hand flashing in the sunlight.

Then peering closely, the village folk spotted a halo. They didn't know that during the months of digging and then after the accident, when he lay crippled and unconscious, Pekalov's hair had turned gray; they only saw the white light above his head, saw that the young Pekalov was running and shouting to them and rejoicing.

No one from the village ever saw him again. Several women confirmed that they then witnessed two angels flying down to the young Pekalov, his head graced by a halo, and the angels took him by the arms and carried him away into the sky. But in a hundred years, when roads were laid out and when on that same side of the river a small country town grew up, a connecting bridge appeared, at first wooden, then next to it, at the entrance to the bridge, a chapel. On the wall there was a depiction of the event. Until recent times you could see the picture—never mind that it was faded—and make out that angels were lifting a man to heaven. The angels were drawn with both arms and wings. The body of the person flying up with their assistance was tipped back a little to the side, because it wasn't as easy for the angel on the left to hold the one-armed man as for the angel on the right.

4

There exists an opinion that a state of delirium creates highly individualized expression, but not in an intimate or strictly personal sense. In fact, its value is in its exposure—or release—of self-knowledge, down to the very depths of genetic memory. In other words, you contain more than you yourself have accumulated. This opinion holds that in a state of delirium, freed from the censorship of your own age, you're capable of perceiving and even hearing the past, and even beyond that—living within it.

However, when put to a test, the present doesn't let a person go that easily, the present is tenacious. (Banality is more than willing to stand guard.) So in fact it occurred that one person in a severe state of shock didn't live at all in the past; this person imagined himself to be not his own ancestor, not a brook, not a bird on a sage bush—he imagined himself to be a lightning rod! (Developing the right image is not a high priority for a deranged consciousness.) Whatever the options, he considered himself to be a modern lightning rod and that, naturally, he was shining on the roof above a house, like a glistening sword raised by an arm on high.

He lived a vital life; he had a genuine one, that is. He sensed it when at first the storm clouds were just passing by, but then they gathered densely around him, clustering tightly in the air, one on top of another. The clouds grew heavy. Rain sprinkled down. The first short flash came then, but it missed! (At this point it's important to understand the sensation he felt: he both yearned for lightning and feared it.) Then more flashes, and they came closer and closer to the house on which he stood. He huddled in a state of fear combined with a kind of sweet languor, and his little casement of a body trembled.

Finally, there came the expected and precise strike. It cut him to the bone. Feeling a severe, sharp pain pass through his body, he thought that he would die and that death would be a joy. Another blow followed. And again he allowed a flash followed by pain to pass through his slender spine. He was perspiring heavily. And at the same time, thirsting for more, he cried out to the lightning and called it down again on himself. "Come again! Hit me!" He called the clouds back and truly regretted the sight of the sky clearing and the storm disappearing. Then it seemed to him that he hadn't received his fair share, hadn't got what he had coming in life.

In post-surgery intensive care he lay right next to me, one cot next to the other. When a storm was gathering beyond the hospital windows, he was the first to catch a scent of the electricity in the air. Once Nurse Olya was drawing the curtains when he shouted, "Come over here! To me!"

Nurse Olya, who was sometimes pleasant and sometimes cross, suppressed a laugh and answered, "Here we go again. As if I didn't have enough to do without you!"

But he wasn't shouting either to her or to us: the poor guy was shouting to the storm clouds and was calling the lightning down. That's the way he called the lightning. Later his mind recovered and he left intensive care before the rest of us and was already walking. He roamed around the hospital, peering in everywhere. He badgered the nurses and mercilessly swallowed pills, which is how he got his nickname. He was twenty-nine. He had a tumor on his spine, and it was spreading, but not in the most dangerous direction. He had several operations.

Two years later one of my fellow patients from the hospital called and said that the *pill popper* had been *laid to rest,* and something snapped inside me—that kind of snap that comes with a loss. No matter what you lose, it disappears according to a simple, uncomplicated scheme: it once was and it is no more—until it's lost irretrievably, to the point of incomprehension. But the incomprehension is in us. I tried to find out whether the *pill popper* had died a painful death.

"A breeze. In his sleep."

I only remember how he wandered through the halls of the hospital, asking for the little white pills, and how nurses would tell him that he wasn't keeping track of how many he was taking, that there's a chemical effect that's harmful. "Show some willpower," they'd say. "Just endure it."

And he would answer with a glowing face and a sly, cute little grin, "And what if it hurts like hell?"

I wasn't very different from him when, recovering from shock and sedated with morphine, I became delirious, but I didn't consider myself either a poplar tree or a ravine, not a wolf cub and not the digger of a tunnel—neither Pekalov nor a hopeless drunk. Genetic memory was silent. I sometimes considered myself the mobile bed of a dump trunk, but most often of all, a jet fighter—a YK-77—with a broken wing and trying to land, but never able to—just no way! That's the way it was: either a lightning rod or a fighter plane. (The pretentious, senseless effort at creating an image is a totally modern feature of the phenomenon.)

Even during the recovery stage, when the worst was past and it was possible to move around, at least on crutches, again one day I started to insist that I was a YK-77, that I was about to land after surviving a skirmish with only one punctured wing. "Now this is a piece of cake. This time I'll make it—no sweat." I don't remember whether I ate during those days, whether I talked to fellow patients in the ward, but I do remember perfectly the way the surgeon, as he removed still another soiled bandage from the wound, yelled, "You head for one more landing and I'll send you flying off to the mental ward!"

In fact, the psych ward was called the Special Unit for Trauma Victims.

It was then that out of memory the simple legend of Pekalov turned up. Just then that it rose up, pursuing me, trying to lure me. I wanted to merge with that world, to mingle with its ordinary people (my genetic memory was trying to heal me), but then I lost the trail, wasn't able to enter that former time, and once again imagined myself as a YK jet fighter monotonously circling a landing strip. I didn't know how to make my way into the old story I had known since childhood: the past first pestered, then dodged me. It remained the past, always awaiting my first step in the right direction, only immediately to go silent; the past was fearful and elusive, demonstrating that there would be no return and that it had gone silent in me earlier than I realized. What a huge number of words I had acquired and pronounced without it!

"Olya!" I yelled in torment. Not only was I in pain, but also it seemed important to convey at least to her, a harried nurse, that I understood something essential—that I shouldn't be afraid to tell my pain, shouldn't to be afraid to make it all-embracing, to make my loss universal. At that moment I understood that I would be deluding or even deceiving myself if I held back and didn't slough this off me and dump it on everyone living (not, of course, to settle mutual scores with someone or something).

For an instant the past again approached and lured me, and I held a shovel with an old-fashioned shape and dug the earth. The digging reminded me—or only wanted to remind me—of the flow of life, in which, for lack of a bridge or a big, hollow tunnel, I went another way. I went struggling through the tunnel path, through the hole, twisting left and right. I took some kind of too intricate, excessively zigzagging steps at a time when I needed only to wait it out. I didn't know how to wait and didn't want to, even for my own experience (to show me the way?), and it's not surprising that very soon I didn't even know my directions, I got turned around (in the dark and with only one candle)—but the river flowed on; the river was above me, I heard its noise and wasn't afraid of the noise, but I no longer knew which way it was flowing, which way was with the current, which way was against, and which way was across; I had meandered so that in the darkness there remained only one thing to do: to dig; to dig as far as necessary, no matter what extra labor and losses were required, I had to get out to the other, untrampled shore. But this, it seems, was impossible.

"Olya!" I called as I lay on the hospital cot, in delirium after the trauma.

But Pekalov continued digging. Yes, there was this feeling that he went on digging even when he became invisible to people, and that even for that reason maybe, the angels carried him up, that the ascension didn't change anything—he remained in the same place, with his shovel. This is a matter of opinion. As everyone knows, young people are too trusting of the imagination, and old people are too afraid of death, but if you're not young and not old and if, as a rule, you possess a sense of balance and if you, nevertheless, don't lapse into excessively exaggerated moods, then what use would you have of some Pekalov? And I kept trying (now with effort) to imagine him, how his muscles strain and he tosses the dirt back and claws into the rubble when a rage seizes him.

Not then nor now do I want Pekalov and all his obstinacy reduced to just a bare human thought, large and capacious perhaps, but weakly expressed and without flavor— without a dark, overhanging arch, without a scraping of shovels and without falling drops of water. What need do I have of this *without?* I wanted to see him, the living Pekalov, but only once through the thickness of time did I see him. He stood, leaning against his shovel, bent over because of the low arch of the tunnel, up to his knees in mud. He had both hands, but lumps of earth had fallen inside his collar, and he had stopped digging in order to brush his back and shake off the lumps of dirt that had tumbled down on him. The face is tired. Nearby, on a pile of gravel, stands not a candle but a kerosene lamp. However, like any vision, he had few words to say. In a leisurely way he stopped brushing off his back, and, looking amazed at me and my presence (for him I was another one of the newcomers), he said, "There's no time . . . Whatta you want from me?"

And turning my back to him, I continued to dig farther.

The hospital settled down to sleep. A nurse went from ward to ward with everything for the nightly injections. I saw her white smock appear and again disappear—and finally she left; there wasn't a soul in the long hospital corridor. It was night. Autumn. Outside the windows a gentle rain fell. The windows of the corridor were lighted, and in their reflection I saw myself hobbling along in parallel. A patient with my face walked on crutches—the appearance was fragile and shaky, but looking through my own face, from the height of the fourth floor I could see out to an asphalt path, wet and glistening from the rain. Then something else, quite apart, caused me to look more closely. An apartment building stood opposite the hospital and also there on the fourth floor, among a multitude of darkened windows, one was lighted, and inside a little girl of about ten was standing (I noticed her immediately); pressing herself up against the window and sticking her face to the glass, she was waving desperately. Her face was frightened.

I hobbled down the corridor about fifty feet, observing out of the corner of my eye her little figure in the window. And when I stopped for a minute to shift my crutches, the little girl waved more forcefully, so there was no doubt—she was waving to me.

Something was wrong over there and the little girl was signaling for help. Could it be she's locked in? For some reason she can't bang on the door. (Or is she scared? Maybe someone's threatening her?) And since it's the fourth floor she can't break the window and jump out. It's possible that besides me, ambling along the hospital corridor, no one, not a soul, sees her and can help her; otherwise why would she wave and call to me—a man on crutches—for help? She was little and thin—helpless-looking. But how to help if, since the doors in our hallway were never opened, I couldn't even shout to her? And my legs were shaking—I was already tired. I could barely drag one foot after the other. Very few days had passed since I'd had two operations. I sat down, almost crashing into an old armchair on wheels. Rickety and with its wheels long ago rusted out, now it stood immobile day and night in the hospital corridor and was used by patients for resting when, on crutches like me, they tired out midway along such a long hallway.

Still, I needed to get up and go, even though going down to the first floor on crutches was not at all easy. (The girl's desperate signals, her face pressed up against the window made me hurry.)

Once I reached the bottom floor, I hid. On one side was the main hospital entrance, where I heard the voice of the coatroom attendant, who was discussing something with a doctor. Here I needed to go totally unnoticed. Fortunately, on the other side there was a door barred off, but with a hatchway. I looked—no one was around. I put my crutches close beside the totally closed-off door and crawled into the hatch. At first I didn't make it. The cast attached to my waist allowed me to crawl through the hatchway only if I first lay down on the floor. I lay down. I crawled through. Already scenting the rain and hearing its patter on the other side, I lay down again and with one hand dragged the crutches one at a time toward me through the hatch. Pulling myself up, I started hobbling as fast as I could. As I crossed the area between the hospital and the apartment building in the rain, I waved hastily from time to time to the little girl, as if to say, "I'm coming." And when I quickly appeared outside the sagging hospital fence, she also waved, happily but with a look of great fear, as if on my crutches I was coming too late and could only barely manage to get there in time to help. I rushed, but I was already out of breath.

I counted the windows, but anyway it was possible to make a mistake. I went in the building entrance and started going up the stairs, but somehow the floors were undefined, with stairs going up three flights rather than the usual two. This worked out to be first a half-floor, then a floor and a half, and two and a half. I didn't know whether the fourth floor was located at a higher or lower level than the fourth floor of the hospital. Also, I didn't know which door to start knocking on, ringing the doorbell, or maybe even forcing open.

I thought immediately of knocking with my crutch on every door, one after the other, but in the midst of a general hubbub at night, when people would wake up and start running and yelling, it might be impossible to hear the little girl and to lose her. It was easy to be mistaken. Especially given the fact that on the fourth floor (or the third and a half) the corridor veered sharply to the right and then abruptly down-ward—displaying the design of an old building where there were all kinds of apartments, scattered out from each other. I hobbled deeper inside. There were three more apartments, but I thought it unlikely that these apartments were the last ones. At that point the end of the hall suddenly widened, and at the corner there appeared an adjoining hallway, which turned sharply to the left and downward, away from me. Beyond the turn I could make out a new extension of the hall, no longer with windows in the end wall, somehow connecting to a half-basement. Never had I been in such a nest of communal apartments. Apartments were partitioned off everywhere—apartments as well as various pipes and the odors of a half-basement. I was obviously off track, had got-ten turned around, and to knock on doors here would be a mistake, of course. I was worn out. My legs had played out, and the rubbing of the crutches under my arms was causing a strong, sharp pain. *The finest crutch won't run far,* so they say. I stopped. In the gloom of the corridors (a few glimmers of light had already appeared) there was the strong smell of earth, and I saw that the corridor went down deeper and deeper. The arches on the side were already earthen. And the ceiling above also earthen. In places there was clay. I stopped again: I spotted a drop trickling down from the ceiling and falling under my feet. And then I heard up above me a noise: the sound of a river was there. The river ran quietly and evenly. Arches overhead, earth and someone's candle by my feet—suddenly everything jerked, switching into another rhythm, and it all started swimming . . .

Even with delirium, even when the past was squeezing itself in, the hospital corridor belonged to the real world. I glanced out the window: I saw a streetlight with its flat, frosted shade gradually filling up with rain. It was nighttime, a slow autumn rain was falling, there was a building opposite the hospital with one lighted window. And a little girl with her hands up against the pane was gazing out. And her small face was distorted with pain. *This* was reality.

And then I hobbled off into the real. There wasn't a soul in the hospital corridor, and, shifting my crutches, I shuffled along the linoleum in my leather house slippers. How much slower and more difficult the going was now! Moreover, in the real world one had to be more circumspect. (Knowledge of the hospital was a knowledge of rules and back doors.) As a preliminary I went into my own ward, a corner one and the farthest from the elevators. Under my hospital gown I put on a light sweater (thinking of the rain) and changed from hospital pajamas to jogging pants with white stripes. And moving toward the door I took several ten-ruble bills from what money I had and stuck them in my pocket, just in case. One of my ward-mates was sleeping, the other one was lying down and staring at the ceiling, not reacting at all, either to my arrival or my bustling about as I changed clothes. His shirt was unbuttoned at the chest, as if he were suffocating. I left the room—the finest crutch won't run far—and went down the darkened stairway, one flight after another, to the first floor.

Only the main entrance of the hospital was closed, it was empty and dark there, but the back door that I needed was open, a light was on, a dim bare bulb, and a little guy in a padded peasant jacket was on duty and smoking. He yawned lazily when I hobbled past. When I had already passed through the strip of light and tobacco smoke, he mumbled something like, "Only don't you be gone long now . . . " I moved right along, placing the crutches on the wet asphalt, on the wet grass. My legs were weak and shaking. My mouth had become dry. But the rain was warm. I passed beyond the sagging fence, and after the air of the hospital the thick smell of wet trees hit me in the face. The apartment building was a stone's throw away. I saw the little girl in the window, mouthing words silently, moving her lips. The building entrances (in reality) were on this side, and I was easily able to calculate the distance by counting the number of windows from the corner of the building, and knew which entrance to take. Craning my neck, I checked the window where she was, just to make sure, and went in. As I climbed the stairs I started breathing faster. My crutches tapped along the hallway. The building was the most ordinary kind, with the usual arrangement of floors, the usual number of apartments—four—on each landing, this was normality, everyday life, the prosaic interior of an apartment building, and on one floor a door was open. When I went in, I saw it was a service area, lined with pipes. The entrance hall led not to rooms, but somewhere away to the side. I ventured in a bit, looked up—the ceiling was covered with boards: earth. I stopped. And saw that again it was dripping. And at once I heard that same sound overheard: the sound of the river . . .

Within about a year's time a couple of dozen patients had come and gone from our ward; one of them was an old man, a Turk. After the trauma he was in that state of primitive, uncensored shock; he didn't see himself either as a lizard, a sand dune, a dervish, or a mullah. He suffered from a modern and rather common delusion; he considered that all clocks and watches had gone wrong and that they had to be destroyed because they give false time. He was mainly silent, and if he spoke at all it was about ruined watch mechanisms, about wheels and springs. His forty-year-old daughter, a manicurist, often came to see him.

I remember that it took me a while, but eventually I found a way we could communicate. I drew clock faces with arrows on pieces of paper; he would collect them and with great glee would tear them to shreds—he was destroying clocks, if not time itself. Nurse Olya and her assistant were grateful to me, since after tearing up dozens of pieces of paper with clock faces drawn on them, he would be in an excellent mood and ate dinner without tantrums, without throwing dishes out the window. We got along well. Our beds were opposite each other; he tore up clock faces while I drew new ones; I also got satisfaction of my own from this process, because at the very bottom of the drawings, in minuscule letters too small to be noticed by the doctors, I signed them "YK-77."

5

(There wasn't one Alexander the Great in the psych ward, neither a Napoleon nor anyone like either of them.)

There is a parable about Alexander the Great—about how he broke some beautiful object— an amphora, it seems. He threw the wonderful and delicate object on the ground because he couldn't take it with him on his long journey. Under the conditions of his expedition, sooner or later the amphora would have broken, but he had already come to like it and was accustomed to it. His gesture illustrated his regret: he didn't want to love it and didn't want to lose it. In a certain sense, all people resemble the great young warrior. We live just that way—breaking and discarding the past. We must travel lightly on our journeys, eat and drink until suddenly we miss something and then start to bawl, "The loss— oh, the loss!"

It's even surprising that amid all the legends about Alexander this one, too, was preserved. There's nothing especially remarkable about it; in fact, this is exactly the way people live. One can imagine how many vases—and more than vases—Alexander the Great destroyed. Aristotle was his teacher, of course, but one must assume that the philosopher often threw up his hands in despair at his rowdy but prestigious pupil, whom he had to tolerate.

The human being's spirit doesn't live and breathe according to all that he loves; this is only one side of the coin. There's another. For, if people century after century discard the things they love out of fear of becoming too attached to them, if they break their vases and amphorae, then can they cry out about fate?

The problem isn't that the return trip lacks aesthetics. One could make one's peace with that. Life is directed at specific goals, and the roads on the way back are littered not only because on his way to a confrontation with the present the person ate, drank, discarded tin cans, and so forth.

Leo Tolstoy, who disliked Alexander the Great, also asked why we understand the past so poorly or don't even understand it at all. He appealed for attention to the loss, but in fact he was answered in quite a contemporary way. "Yes," those who answered his appeal said. "Monuments of the past have to be preserved. Look, we're painting churches, we're reprinting ancient books." Tolstoy was speaking about understanding, but he was answered with talk of museums. He had in mind the human being; those who replied only wanted to know whether the tombstone over the dead man's head was pretty or not. He spoke, but they didn't listen. In the end this became tiresome for him.

"The past must soar by itself, like a bird," one man at a dinner party answered without knowing the provocative story about Alexander and the broken vase.

He said "soar" as if to avoid saying that a bird simply "flies up." But the sense of his remark was clear.

THE LOSS

I was reminded of the pale, gray-haired old man who long, long ago used to wander with short little steps around the clotheslines in the courtyard. It was the usual apartment courtyard. It was summer. The old man had been retired for many years. Roaming around, he came up and winked as if he wanted to show us something on the sly. He kept one hand mysteriously in his pocket. And sure enough, he pulled an unusual bird out of his pocket. True, it was an ordinary sparrow, but when this sparrow flapped its wings it didn't fly away. The old man held it in his palm, and we boys marveled as we looked closely, inspecting the bird, but its wings weren't broken, its legs weren't tied, and in general everything was fine. The sparrow chirped briskly. No one, not even the old man, knew why the sparrow didn't fly away. It was that way when he found it and picked it up.

The noisy and drunken dinner party was in full swing. I was fourteen, and sitting next to me and raising his vodka glass was an elderly bookkeeper, a lively man with the air of a village philosopher. Amid the general din he started a conversation about individual endeavors and their appreciation by posterity.

No one was listening to him, so he kept repeating his story. When a certain monkey rose up on two legs for the first time, the story went, his fellow monkeys, with squeals and grimaces, scoffed at the futility of his effort. To stand up took considerable effort; it was complicated and even painful for the body and its muscles. They teased him, "Weirdo! Do you really think that posterity will remember you?" It turned out to be true—he wasn't remembered. That was the whole joke—that a daring and smart monkey wasn't appreciated. He was forgotten. Truly forgotten! The old village bookkeeper had lived a long time and had traveled a great deal in his time. He had carried on conversations in airplanes, in trains, in cars, in streetcars, he had talked to people everywhere—on ferryboats, on farm wagons, even on horseback as he rode side by side with someone. But in all these conversations not one person had said a word of praise for the first monkey to stand up on two legs. Not once. Descendants don't remember. They forget . . .

A plate of homemade sausage lay on the table. The hosts themselves had prepared it all themselves—stewed and ground the meat, applied the seasonings, tasted it and stuffed it into the sausage skin. A decanter of vodka stood beside the sausage, and when the decanter was poured Aunt Darya leaned forward and clinked glasses with Viktor Sergeyevich. They were cousins, and the entire family had decided that they should be seated next to each other, so they could settle their quarrel. Viktor Sergeyevich, taking the opportunity to make friendly gestures, kept repeating to Aunt Darya, "Hey, neighbor, why aren't you drinking?" To which she answered that she was drinking right along, in fact that already *something was skipping in her chest.*

But he kept encouraging her to have more. "Never mind about your chest. You have to make your eyes skip!"

Farther around the table there was Uncle Pavel with his handsome, intelligent face. Then his wife, Anna Vasiliyevna. And there was Uncle Kesha—missing his left arm, but with eight wounds and three medals. He got disabled from a shell while he was sitting beside his own cannon and pounding on a nail in his boot. His wife had died recently. Uncle Kesha sat quietly, having already downed with his one hand ten glasses of vodka, and he couldn't have any more. He didn't hear the story about the money, he didn't hear about the cousins kissing and making up, he didn't hear anything. Surrounded by the noise of the party, he sat whispering something to himself. "A so-ong! We want a song!" people here and there yelled.

Beyond Uncle Kesha, beyond Uncle Pavel, and at an angle across from Anna Vasiliyevna sat Uncle Seryozha, a peculiar man. He thrashed his kids in out-of-the-ordinary ways, but also he had passionately tortured his wife, even displaying a talent for it, so that she twice had tried to kill herself. "A so-ong!" he now yelled. Always busy with something, Uncle Seryozha was the loud and energetic initiator of many projects, which he then tossed aside half-finished. His itch to be busy with something led him to get involved in some shady deals, major in scope for our village, but then he got cold feet and ran to the police to confess. The outcome was that his neighbor and partner in the matter got sent to prison for two years. Uncle Seryozha got off clean. While the investigation was still under way, he approached his neighbor's wife and pleaded for money. "Otherwise I'll tell the whole truth and they'll lock him up," he said, and, wringing her out for all she was worth, he took one big ruble bill after another from her, but at the trial he opened up with answers to everything that they asked and didn't ask. He carried himself proudly in court. "Comrades, I've thought it all over. My conscience came to me on time. Be what there may, but my conscience hasn't withered away." His neighbor got five years, which later somehow they knocked down to two, but he got off with a fine, almost all of which he paid out of the neighbor's hush money. Before the trial, as part of the deal, he got the neighbor's wife to sleep with him. A smooth talker, pushy and calculating, he told her over and over, "Otherwise I'll tell the whole truth at the trial." The neighbor's wife didn't have much money, so he told her, "Pay with some hard currency— the bed will do." When the neighbor got sent up for two years, he used alcohol to train the wife to go to bed with him. Later, sitting in the only village beer joint, next to the bathhouse, he recounted some of the woman's bedroom idiosyncrasies. "She likes me," he explained. "But myself, I dump *that kind*. I sampled it—and back to normal."

At the party Uncle Seryozha was yelling loudly, demanding his favorite song, but in five years he would die of cancer; then the noise of the long family party table (and the old bookkeeper's drunken philosophizing about the monkey) would echo in him in a strange way. On his deathbed Uncle Seryozha would call his wife. And he would call his children. And he, too, would ask, "Can it be that I won't stay in your memory? Is it possible you'll forget me?"

He would cry a bit. He would know that he was dying. He would call his wife closer—the wife he had beaten and tortured and who twice tried to kill herself, and—now not in the children's presence—he would ask her bitterly, "Is it possible you'll forget me, Nina?"

And he would die. And—not remain in her memory. Because Nina would forget his evil—his vicious taunts, his twisted mind. But she would remember and grieve for quite a different person, it would seem, although one with the same last name, the same first and middle names. Remembering him, Auntie Nina would sigh, "Oh, yes. I had a husband, he's dead already. He was a good man. Tender . . . "

But then comes the peal—that special and frightening swelling of sounds when the lungs seize an excess of air in order to raise the sonic pressure, step by step, right up to the sky: so, *end-less-ly the thun-der di-id ri-in-ng* . . . When they reach the heights the singers sail on to the end. Their supply of air is exhausted. Their eyes seek one spot to rest on just as the voices reach the breaking point: *di-id ri-in-ng.* The sounds soar powerfully beyond all limits, the faces, exhausting all the possibilities of the moment, release a smile—satisfaction and joy: we can do it, you bet we can, that's us singing. The female voices rise, running ahead, now to the right, now to the left, but they don't overtake the others. Enormous fields and open spaces merge into a point. That's us. So let them forget us! Forget us entirely. This is us, while we're still living. *Is it possible they will forget?* The song winds down, but the refrain resounds with meaning, like the open spaces themselves.

Fierce in their battles they did fall
Their swords still sheathed, warriors a-all . . .

On the fourth day everything goes into decline. Everyone's lying down, worn out, nursing hangovers, stretched out here and there, one beside the other . . . They would get up, gulp something down, munch on a half-dead cucumber, chew loudly, smoke—then stretch out again. But how wonderful those first three days were! What a feast they had, how they yelled, how they kissed, whether as cousins or not, and how they sang!

6

To *dig* some more—I was eleven: a time of famine, the summer was stressful, and given the circumstances, my mother needed to pack me off somewhere, but where to?

At her wit's end about how to cope, she sent me—a level-headed kid—to a boarding home for the blind, which was overseen and managed by a distant, near-blind relative of ours. I was there, of course, illegally. And the whole summer I sponged off the blind. A girl from a poor family was also there, also a sponger. There were only the two of us kids, sluggish and with shrunken stomachs, and maybe what we got from their communal pot wasn't so very noticeable. What's more, we—the girl and me—almost immediately got a crush on each other and because of that we ate almost nothing.

The blind people, who were brought there from the whole district or maybe even the entire region, lived, in fact, on that other side of the river, although a little farther down, where Pekalov's tunnel had come out. The river was the same, and the two blind men who first got out through the tunnel and landed in the marsh had perished in this vicinity; and in any case, during that *long* night it's possible they managed to reach this same area and wander along this very bank as they floundered in the water and cried out for help.

The girl and I spent a day along the river, swimming, strolling in the woods, and even quarreling, because Sashenka, as she was called, didn't keep it a secret that the previous year she had already been in love—with her classmate Tolya.

As an eleven-year-old boy, I only sighed nobly. "I under-stand. This was serious for you . . . " But soon I changed sharply; I wasn't so noble, and even while it was still just barely apparent that Sashenka and I also loved each other and that this was serious, I started being jealous of her past, unfairly eliciting details from her or flying off at her and say-ing, "Well, why don't you just go off to him!"

During the summer the half-blind manager of the home called me aside two or three times and in the concerned tone of a relative asked, "Well, how's it going?"

To which, hemming and hawing with embarrassment, I answered, "It's going fine."

"And how are you sleeping?"

"I'm sleeping well."

"And how's the food?"

"Fine . . . "

I was afraid that he'd caught wind of something about our romance. In the evening Sashenka would come to the leaky tent assigned to me on the outskirts of the grounds. She was cautious in coming, and we would kiss just in the evening, in the dark and only once a day, assuming as we did that to kiss any more than that would be to behave like adults. We sat in the tent and ten feet away the waves of the Ural splashed. I had already started smoking then, and when I did, I made sure to tug the tent flap shut, but the smoke seeped out anyway, and Sashenka would walk around for a while near the tent to let me know in case someone noticed. As soon as I tossed away the butt, we would sit down side by side and be silent for a long time. There was only the sound of the river, and like orphans we quietly listened to the beat-ing of the waves. Or at times, just the calm, measured lap-ping of waves against the bank. And through the tent flap we would watch a path of moonlight shining on the river.

The blind people, of course, amazed us. For example, at those times when I would be on my way to find Sashenka to call her down to the river, or when she might be on her way to my tent from the cook's room, where she was quartered, I would be walking along the bank, and suddenly someone would call out to me, "Nikolai?" but I would keep walking, since I wasn't Nikolai. But Sashenka said that when they called out to her, she would freeze, and for a while the blind man would listen again keenly. He would realize he had mistaken the sound of the steps and would call again, "Oh . . . Seryozhka! Why didn't I recognize you the first time?" But neither was I Seryozhka and, keeping silent, I went on my way; however, if this happened to Sashenka, she again would freeze and with her heart pounding would run fast farther up the bank. The blind man would stand and stare in that direction.

There were about fifteen of them, and for two children, it was hard to avoid them, as the manager had warned us to do from the first day. He said that the blind people took to other people readily and were overjoyed at the arrival of any new person; for that reason we needed to avoid them. The manager was afraid that just because of their friendliness, they would start to ask questions and eventually might find out, straight from us, that we were living off them, eating out of their pot. In short, there was an agreement to skirt around them. They wandered along the sandbanks forlornly or just sat juggling pebbles, and when I went past not only did they hear my footsteps, but even heard me breathing. They sensed that I smoked. "Nikolai . . . Come over closer!" There were three smokers among them, they all knew who they were, and they called me by those same names. Sashenka was lighter than me, and her footsteps were so soft that the blind people didn't always call out to her, but rather, taking her for a bird, just followed her path with their unseeing eyes.

In bad weather when the Ural splashed noisily against the shore, they would gather suddenly on the bank and stand in a state of excitement, swaying together at the very edge of the wet sand. Waves rolled in at their feet. Fixing their clouded eyes on the other side of the river, the blind people gazed out in silence (somehow they also were expecting salvation), and they would stand that way for hours, craning their necks and peering out as the river washed wave after wave upon them. Something there beckoned them.

We ate separately, and for that reason I didn't see and don't remember how they ate, how they passed the plates around to each other. But on the other hand, we saw them go many times down to the river when it was flowing quietly and gently, when there was an endless blue sky with the sun like a great ball in the middle and the heat made it the best time to go into the water. They would always go in at one particular spot—probably where there were fewer rocks and they knew there had to be a sandy bottom. The river was shallow near the shore, so the blind people had to wade for a long time. They were impatient, but as they waded out they stretched out in a line, one after the other; however, in the deep spots, where the river was dark blue, they would help Kiryusha. He was a fat man, possibly suffering from dropsy; flabby and shuddering with fear, he was visibly the opposite of all of them, who were lean and well built. In the deep water they would stop, bunch together, even squeezing in close on each other, then help the fat blind man get in the water. Fearful of falling, he would whimper and slide in. Then bumping against them with his inflated belly, he would move along the line from one to the other, with a hand widespread to grab hold of each next person. But having passed him from hand to hand out to the deep water, they would then make him pay for their trouble. "Now swim, Kiryusha. Don't try to go any farther!" It's hard to say whether he was weak-minded or just couldn't swim well. The Ural River is famous for its drownings, but that year almost one person after another drowned. Kiryusha was afraid. He splashed loudly like a whale, but didn't move a foot farther than the little space indicated to him.

After swimming far out into the river the blind people

broke into little groups, probably just to talk, but maybe to consult each other about getting back safely to the bank. They often craned their heads around, as if trying to orient their wet faces as exactly as possible to the light. However, they knew well where the shore was and possibly were just holding their faces and eyes up to the sun. They clustered together as they swam, either two or three men together or a man and woman. There were only two women in all among them—pretty, young, and blind. Both the men and the women always swam in the nude.

They would return slowly at first, wandering through the shallow water, then stopping at the very bank. Two or three came back at a time, not waiting for the others—they would stop for a moment, still nude, in order to take the first step onto the bank from the shallow water. The rippling waves still tickled the leg that remained in the water, but the leg that reached out for the bank shook as it tested the solid ground. Once firmly on the shore, they remembered again that they were blind and that a pebble can be sharp and any bush an obstacle. Already on solid ground, *he* stood on guard, and now *she* took her first step. They had made it. They stood on the bank, wiping the water off each other, tanned and laughing, and suddenly their laughter stopped, and for a short time again they cast their eyes, clouded over and white, on the river—to the other side, to the shore that troubled them.

7

Personal misfortunes are personal: they are delicate and difficult to grasp and it's better to keep them to yourself. But what are you to do if it's impossible to understand everything based on your own limited, one-sided experience?

When I saw the digger through time, he stood leaning on his shovel and replied to me that he was in a hurry, that it was time for him to get on with his digging. He was standing in the tunnel. His lamp burned dimly. And I remember: he said that he was rushing. But maybe he also *saw* me? And maybe it was oppressive for him in his tunnel and he wanted to understand me just as much as I did him. Maybe he saw me through the thick layers of days and years, and there he stood, leaning on his shovel, and he watched an injured, delirious man lying on his hospital cot with his face up and unable to turn over. Possibly at that instant we wished each other the same thing, I relying on his insight and strength, and he on mine, but both helpless, and this was the determining factor in our touching across time. He was digging a tunnel and I lay in delirium. Because this encounter was unexpected, we both were on guard. We didn't have time to rejoice. Each of us remained closed in our own world, and this was the main fact about our brief encounter. We met . . . Our deepest selves kept silent, not admitting either the mutual fear or the apprehension of contagion from the other's feelings, which forced themselves straight on through the wall of centuries.

"I'm in a hurry. Gotta dig . . . What do you need from me?"

And he grew silent, but then I wasn't demanding a thing, not even hoping for something, I just wanted a word or at least a gesture, that's all, and even this wasn't just for my own sake. There wasn't in me a trace of any carefully concealed desire to interfere in another person's life.

For the moment I waited for this noncontact to turn into something or to change to some other mode: no matter what the silence, a bundle of purposeful efforts had been set in motion and then had withdrawn into themselves. As a patient I believed this, not only because of my physical incapacity, but also because of the blind alley I found myself in, a dead end that I, like anyone, wanted to avenge wherever I could. It may be wrong and even shameful to retreat from one's own reality, but the psyche itself performs its own release through metamorphosis, when it can no longer bear the pain.

And it was not the self's expression of compensation for certain disappointments. Pekalov commanded only as much of the earth as he could hold in the palm of one hand. He was too much of a trader to be a hero, too shallow and inconsistent for a fanatic, too rebellious to be a total loser. In every way he was not comparable to such types, although by his stubborn digging he was like them all: he confirmed the mystery of human nature, which reveals itself only at those minutes when the human being unshackles himself.

But common sense hoots at this. "What mystery? Nonsense!" it says. "It's entirely possible that there wasn't anything to all this, expect for that tale of the shaggy, bowlegged monkey who climbed down from the tree and started walking on two legs, only because that made it easier and quicker to stuff his belly. It's altogether possible that your Pekalov is just one of your writer's whims. Subconsciously everybody's willing to become a wise man like you and think that only the past is alive and vibrant. And then our own times become something special only when they've passed."

8

A man—over forty, his name doesn't matter—stops in the middle of a field, then steps to the side, changing his angle of perspective, and—looks.

He is searching for a certain confluence of things. This moves him deeply, because hundreds of years ago the people who chose this spot stood exactly this way and looked in the same direction. The fact can be vouched for that they saw just what he sees—definitely *they,* because the place for settling a village is not chosen by any one person. The man who was over forty and whose name is unimportant approached from the side, where the road runs, and one must assume *they* also came from that direction, although there was no road there then.

They saw these same two low mountains, one worn down by time, but the other with a more or less sharp peak. They also saw two creeks flowing together. No, more exactly, they saw only the Marchenovka, which then had no name, but they saw it and someone said, "Look, the whole creek is in a grove of trees. Won't it dry up?" "Why should it dry up? The trees are green!" someone else answered. And they went up closer to the creek along this path (the path wasn't there—they walked straight over to it), and only when they were near did they notice the second, quite small little creek—the Berlyuzyak. It joined the Marchenovka, hidden by trees and by the mountain with the tall peak. They went up to the creek and, of course, tasted the water and dug around the tree roots to get an idea of their age and vigor (dependent on the creek water). They came up exactly from that direction, certainly not from the mountain side. Once they saw the second little creek they had to rejoice, surely exchanging looks of surprise. Two! Two little creeks—then it means that one won't dry up—and that could have been decisive in their choice.

The width of the Marchenovka as well as of the Berlyuzyak was nine or ten feet—quite a bit of water, certainly enough for their needs. Then, excited partly by the decision they had already made, they started to take a look around with an eye to settling as families, and maybe there developed a heated staking out of territory. "I'll put up a house here." "Then I'll be over there." Now, looking back, he knew and could say with exact precision who lived where. There weren't many of them. He knew all their last names, adopted from first names or nicknames. He himself bore one of them. While it was strange that the abandoned village had been torn down long ago, rather than distancing him from them, the abandonment and destruction brought him closer, and the fact that he sees the landscape now without cabins, just as they saw it for the first time, creates a first sense of intimacy with them. By studying the place, he was able to know where and how they chose it, and casting a glance around with the past in mind, he could form a picture of the land without cabins, without wattle fences and planted trees.

The trees that once had stood along the road—the main and only street of the village—had long since toppled and fallen, and there remained only those trees that had been there originally—along the creeks. That's the way the land had been—just such a *cabinless* beauty. Exactly as it had also looked to them. One smooth mountain, one with a little peak and slopes along which truck gardens later stretched down to the water.

He saw, so to say, the earth *before* man. A man from the city, he had come here not to mourn over the former village, but just to wander through the place, without a special task or aim, not counting the desire to see it as it was *before*. The little village didn't exist in those distant times, and now, too, it can be said, it didn't exist. And between the first and the second *didn't exist*, the entire life of the village fitted itself in, and together with the village, people's lives were lived and consumed—the fates, passions, births, and deaths of all the players. Even the stage sets of this inconspicuous theater—the family cabin—had been expended. The little village had its birth, its growth, possibly even its time of flourishing; now it lies abandoned, preserving its eternal nonexistence. Then a newcomer enters its afterlife, in a certain ancient sense of the word. So this man born and raised in the city, with children also born and raised there, lives far removed from the life of the little village and has his own subsequent and different life span; however, he turns up here. Is he really alive here? Here, isn't he a man from the afterlife?

The words startled and amused him: the man from the afterlife! Smiling happily and a little lightheartedly, he opens his briefcase and fishes out a bottle. He had brought along a super corkscrew, one that not only opens the bottle but also is designed for the convenience of the drinker, so that after a few sips he can close it, put it back, for instance, in the briefcase until he wants it the next time, all without fear of spilling a drop. The advantage was that he didn't have to drink the whole bottle at once, not overdrink, but could continue to see clearly, walk straight, and, in short, go about life normally at the same time as maintaining an exhilarating high. It was pretty important for him to keep himself at a certain pitch of keen feelings and enjoyment. After taking a swig, he starts down to the creek, as he had planned to go when he viewed it from a distance, down to the place where they had gone—his ancestors, in their moment, in their age.

Tossing the bottle in the briefcase and ambling toward the creek, he walks in their tracks. He goes down, has a smoke, and then, when his sense of light euphoria reaches its peak from drinking the wine in the fresh air, he sings some snatches of a song from childhood; if he finds that he has drunk too little and the intoxication starts to settle, he immediately adds some more. Without surrendering the joyful feeling but also without becoming drunk, he keeps the limits, for he has to return.

Passing under willow trees, he spots a flat rock beside the water, in fact it turns out to be two rocks—white and worn smooth and placed together—where his great grandmother and great-great-grandmother and great . . . would have done the laundry, a woman's lot, a string of intertwined women's faces, women who gave birth and gave birth and gave birth again. (Stretching it a bit, it could be said that they successively all gave birth to him, the man who had come here.) After smoking, he takes a drink from the Marchenovka, cupping the water in his hands and drinking, then he walks up higher—he must sample the Berlyuzyak: it's the same water, but still he has to taste it! This way he extends his enchantment with the place, this is why in essence he even came here, he wants to register himself both here and there—he is a man from the afterlife, one who came down to earth for a couple of days, and he's stretching these days out—nothing surprising in that.

Stretching out even the moments, he sits on a flat rock, smoking a second time, and squints at the quietly flowing

water. And when a tree next to him squeaks over the water—
nn-n-neh . . . nn-neh (in humanized detail—an old willow
moans)—he begins expecting an echo within himself. He
wants a response. (*Neh-neh-n-neh . . .*) The moan grows
louder, fills his ears, but there's no pain, and the expected
tender feeling also doesn't come. What's more, the thought
flashes by that the tree is not at all moaning for the past, it's
moaning as an urgent call. When *they* had come down here
to see whether the water would dry up, the ancestor willow
of this tree squeaked and groaned in exactly the same way,
maybe even more so, in distress, when it barely saw them.
Nature summons, as the female beginning summons in general—she wants communality with a person, she is even
drawn to the person. But when the person comes and the
mutual life begins, it's not exactly what the willow had imagined at the moment of attraction—or it's even completely
different. There are squabbles and quarrels, hurts, but also a
destruction and drying up of the feminine beginning of
nature to a point of infertility. Life is life. However aggravat-
ed by half-lamentable knowledge, the irrational willow
moans again, summoning with her sweetness, calling man in
order to try another time; maybe the willow is even calling
for the last time for him to uproot, plow up, consume,
destroy her, but the poor thing doesn't understand that the
one who has come to her is not man in the usual sense, but a
man from the afterlife.

Birds cawed the first two years in the abandoned village,
or, more exactly, above the village. One year and then another, they squawked (also with moans and complaints) in the
spring, over the land where once there had been fields and
truck gardens, where after the plowing there should be
worms—their food. The birds flew there by habit, as a
domestic cycle, but there was no food. The birds cawed and
cawed for a long time. Then silently flying over to the houses,
they would move from place to place, wherever they discovered ants, spiders, cockroaches—all the bustling small

insects that crawled out of the cracks during the first abandoned spring as soon as the sun warmed them up. They emerge and look for human warmth. The whole year the insects that accompany mankind—our smallest retinue—lived in the deserted village, but then the birds destroyed them. In the second year and the second spring, the birds arrived and again cawed over the fields and garden plots, but not for long. They remembered and flew to the remains of the houses and to their animal barns, cellars, and sheds, but when, all spread out and situated for the kill, they don't find even insects, which were either all eaten up by them before or had frozen during the winter, the birds raise an unusual cry, full of suffering. They sense that this place is no longer inhabited and will not be and that there is no need to come here anymore. They prolong their squawking; it's for the last time. They caw above the abandoned houses, and whoever heard it would confirm just how pained the cries were on their second spring.

Stepping across the rocks, he crossed the Marchenovka, went up the mountain to its very peak. He wanted to stand and look once again, this time from above. From there he saw on a slope of the smooth mountain a noticeable rectangle, almost a triangle, sweeping in the grand scale of its design—the cemetery. There was wild mint and blackthorn there. From here crosses couldn't be made out. Neglected from year to year, the dark green triangle had lost its shape and regularity; first, mint and then blackthorn brush spread together with it; however, like a concession, inside the triangle a whitish bare spot could be seen. In a few more years this bare spot will change considerably, the corners will get rounded off, and the edges will blur even more. Then the triangle of the cemetery, already shifting and distorted by invasive seeds and sprouts, will be transformed into a twisted ring. After that, with a bare spot in the middle formed by light gray sage and the white feathers of steppe grass, the ring will completely split. Only separate green clumps of mint and scattered blackthorn bushes will remain—the form will fade and disappear, and by that time nothing will testify that here people lie or once lay.

He decided to leave the cemetery to the end. Along the Berlyuzyak, where the shadow of a goat path remained, he walked out to the place where once the road crossed the creek; it hadn't grown over, it still crossed it there. The smooth mountain with the dark green triangle of the cemetery shone now against the background of sky, and this reminded him how old man Korol had been carried there to the cemetery. There was a long procession, men carrying the coffin, behind them the old women were scattered out as they shuffled along, farther back the kids walked, and he as a boy stood on at this very spot and listened wide-eyed. The priest from Novo-Pokrovka, a village with a church, had come to conduct the burial rites. A joyful wave of memories of the mountain intensified as one picture after another swept over his mind. At the point where the road crosses the creek, a little before reaching the water, there's a well-packed patch of ground, a kind of swollen spot in the road, a wide place maybe to let other vehicles past, and he and his brother were walking along. "Hey!" came a shout from behind, and they looked around and moved to the side. A wagon harnessed to a team was on its way downhill at a brisk clip—the driver, waving his whip, picked up some speed so that once past the stream, he could fly on wings. "Hey!" He and his brother stepped aside right there at the wide spot in the road (repeating it all, he took one step and another half-step, and again, until it become exact and merged with the past); the wagon rattled, leaving behind a cloud of dust, gathering into a white ball, and he and his brother, squinting, stood in this cloud. The sun baked down on them. The horses and the wagon were already on the other side of the creek, the squeak of wheels and clatter of hooves could be heard from there, but they still stood there and the ball of dust hung in midair.

He was six years old and his brother was five. Maybe five and four. The two boys kept standing there, and the white cloud of dust hung without settling. For forty years now they've been there—two boys squinting through a ball of dust.

He lived here before he started to school, then came on short stays. He spent a summer or two, but after that he essentially forgot the place for many years; he didn't even remember that he came only when there was no place else to go. That's the way it worked out. But perhaps he liked this (reverse) side of coming here: now he was visiting his childhood *in the purest form*. Now he could finish building it and populate its emptiness (with the geography totally intact), especially since there were no new changes. Certainly innovations would have come had the village lived on, but the innovations would have been correlated and assimilated and that's not simple. If the village had still existed, an old man—someone else's grandfather—could be sitting out on the low protective wall around the cabin, quickly aged, dressed in a worn, but modern, city-style sweater of his grandson's (as he squeezed himself back into that time with an identity of its own, he would have to mentally remove the sweater from the old man—so that everything would appear without later attributes). In some village recently he had even seen an old village woman dressed in a skirt and old jeans sitting on the wall around her cabin and eating sunflower seeds.

He moved on, going up the road to the house, or rather to the remains of the house, but for him now it was a house in the sense that radiating from it, several possible routes were interspersed:

you can take the road to the right,

you can take the road to the left,

you can go from the back porch through the garden—
each path has its own charm (or you seek it). The road to the right, of course, has the swollen spot—the patch of road

where two little boys stand in an eternal cloud of dust, but the way through the garden takes you deep inside to a currant bush, grown wild and degenerate, but still *that same* currant bush, and he could pick several berries and chew them, searching in them for *that same* taste. With the currant bush included, that was all—everything that had belonged to him. There was nothing more. Children play at being adults and adults play at being children. But in this case there's something more: he's not playing—he's serious; he's not remembering, he's living it, although none of it belongs to his own life anymore.

According to believers, the man from the afterlife—the spirit that alighted here—is capable of flying above the earth and saying, as he reminds himself, "Here my body went to school; this is where I lived; this is where, sinner, I first copulated with a woman, and here in this big, impressive hospital is where my body died." The man who had come here was luckier in a certain way than the usual spirit flying in from the afterlife, for this place wasn't occupied. There are no new buildings and he sees everything as it is, undisturbed by living people who rush to and fro.

At his great-grandparents' house he sits down on—what to call it?—on a remnant of the foundation, for the house has been torn down. The houses were removed, but their stone foundations—a foot or so wide—still partly jut out from the earth (comfortable now, sir?). If it weren't for the desolation, this would resemble the beginning rather than the end. Viewed from a distance and from above, it would seem that all twenty-five or thirty houses had just begun to be built: the village is small and all the foundations are laid and finished, but the log frames haven't been brought, maybe they haven't cut them yet and that's why they aren't set up on the stone foundations. He looked for a bird in the sky, but there is none, not one. The sky is clear, but from a bird's-eye view (swooping down from a high soaring point) all twenty-five foundations of houses would be now all laid out like a plan, like a *view from above:* you can see the house and inside the house the Russian stove (also a foot high), and beside the cabin an animal shed, and a little ways off, a cellar—everything available. When they needed materials to build other houses in another place, they took everything apart, dismantled the decaying little village down to the bottom, a foot from the ground, but even though they took away the top part the village still exists, but only on a two-dimensional plane. The birds were lost, there's no height, and the sky is limitless: a full triumph of flatness.

He walked past the cellar—it had caved in long ago, and it had been deep; food had been stored there both in winter and summer—an *interment.* Now the pit has collapsed, and if someone should stumble onto it in the dark (he had to leave at night), there would be no unfortunate accident. He sits down again on the ruins of his great-grandparents' walls, now not in order to touch and partake of them, but just to eat. After taking a sip from his bottle, he gets some food from his briefcase. He chews and sits half-turned in order to look down the street, white and dusty—the only street, which threaded the houses together. On the other side there had been a blacksmith's and two long barns built from fine stone: now not two inches were left, not to mention ten. The stones had been hauled away, even dug out of the ground, leaving a shallow outline, already overgrown with weeds. Tall weeds were everywhere. In places the clumps were shoulder high, their only competition for dominance being the eternal stillness and the sagebrush that popped up here and there like giant brooms.

On one of the stones of the foundation, warm from the sun, he sits and eats hard-boiled eggs and tomatoes, big, fleshy, local ones, sprinkling them with salt from a little matchbox, and washing it down with wine. As his stomach gets full and his legs rest after the walk, his thoughts also seem to become satiated, maybe even in a basic sense, actually pretty fitting for a man from the afterlife, whose thoughts from the beginning are broad and expansive. It doesn't matter to him. Also it's easy for him to understand that *they*—three or four of them who long ago planned and began to build a village here—were *fleeing*. In order to come here they had to be leaving someplace else, so eventually someone grieved for the old, familiar place and grumbled at the others. "Where were they dashing off to? We should've stayed put. They're always thinking something up!" People have always grumbled and have always left for new places, there's no stopping them, and they have always even done foolish things along the way. And just why couldn't they reconcile themselves (and their neighbors) to the fact that nature takes a rest from man, understand that the earth is only giving a sigh before they up and dismantle their houses and cart them off. In other, new places they plow and dig wells, hammer posts into hard ground, claw into the clay and rubble, and that's why here now there are sagebrush and tall weeds and oblivion . . . at least here, let the earth take a rest.

He walked slowly along the village: this was where the Korols lived . . . here, the Grushkovs . . . there, the Yarygins . . . there, the Trubnikovs—all relatives. Turning off the road and stepping straight across another ten-inch wall, he turned up as if on a visit to his great-uncle's (his mother's cousin, both with the same grandfather), the man from the afterlife can go in to see him—"Come in, come in. Wipe your feet off over there. He's in the parlor right now." Not a trace remained of the wooden partitions that had stood there. But he can guess the way from the parlor and *correctly* goes in the right door, into the children's room. He can visit his cousin Seryozha and once again see the six-year-old boy die. Seryozha also was brought here for the summer, to breathe the fresh air and drink the country milk, but it came too late and he died within a month from pneumonia. It's no imaginary bed standing there—it's real. Thinking that the little boy wouldn't be comfortable sleeping on a wooden bench, as country folk slept, and that there wouldn't be enough air on the upper level of the great wood stove where the very young and the very old usually slept, Seryozha's mom and dad had brought the factory-made bed with its metal net springs to the village together with him. Now when everything wooden had rotted away, this bed remained the only bed in the village. There it stands—just where it stood before, but each year sinking deeper into the earth; the little boy it belonged to lies there already forty years. The metal net hangs only a foot above the ground; soon it will sink away into the earth and disappear. He felt it with his hand: rusted and corroded, the iron came off the bedposts in whole rings, like a snake skin. In two or three years only the posts will stick up, the net springs will sink and dissolve into dust, and between the bedposts there will be earth.

In winter the Berlyuzyak freezes to the bottom, and snow covers both the foot-high remains of the foundations and the gardens with their still-existing boundary markers; it covers the vestiges of wells and cellars and the little bed with its chain-mail springs. There arises a limit to physical embodiment: the snow is so thick that there's not even a thought of an earlier presence—man has not been here. What a rest for the earth, what happiness! There's a field and several trees. As the willows stand all white in the snow, the blizzard will descend on them like an assault, rushing down through the gardens, utterly heedless of them, and sweep from the smooth mountain onto the plain, there to give full vent to its fury. Until spring itself.

In the summer on the other side of the river—way over there—he and Seryozha saw a gypsy woman who had turned up there, Lord knows why. She didn't approach the village. Either she wanted to stay away from people or she wanted just to be close to an inhabited place at least in case of problems. She went close to the creek, sat down there, and began to give birth. Even in summer Seryozha was all bundled up, and it took him a second to catch his breath, then he explained, "Now a little baby will come out," and all the five kids gathered there waited patiently, standing and watching. The gypsy woman didn't wave them away or yell at them. She went up to the creek and, spreading out a clean cloth, very calmly sat down. A skirt covered everything down to her ankles, so she displayed neither nakedness nor shamefulness. Her face turned red, but not crimson, and she didn't go through any severe torment. It seemed that she didn't once scream out. Finally a small lump of flesh was ejected forcefully, tumbling out with a little thump onto the cloth. As if not wanting to give his mama away with his voice, the baby didn't let out a peep. He'd been well trained. Fussing over him, the gypsy sat down on the grass, then took a *papiroska*, a Russian style-cigarette, from a little bag and lit it. She busied herself with the baby as she smoked—now he was squealing a little. She wrapped him in the cloth, stood up, and left. Only then did she glance at the kids nearby, and he remembers this: she winked at them even with a certain exuberance, as if to say, "This happens in life." No, after smoking she also took a drink of water from the creek; then, carrying the baby, she set out toward the railroad tracks—the direction she had come from, apparently not wanting to go up to the nearest house. She was hurrying to the train . . . Thinking of the train the traveler—over forty and whose name doesn't matter—quickly looked up at the sky: yes, by the time he gets to town and to the hotel it will be dark (he hasn't been to the cemetery yet; he'll do that tomorrow).

He finishes the bottle and tosses it into the weeds, but a second bottle he places in a cool spot by the corner of his grandparents' walls, to be able to drink it when he comes here tomorrow (not to carry it to the hotel). Tomorrow is the last day, and he considers the people he still has to visit in the familiar small town. Which of them to see and how to fit a visit or two into one day, but also to manage to make another trip here, including a stop at the cemetery (there's a certain connection to the bottle left for tomorrow) . . . No, he can't embrace everyone: if he visits one, he'll offend some-one else. In the end, like any visitor, he doesn't have time, and there's also the excuse of not finding someone at home. He cursed when he realized that he hadn't gone a hundred yards before his mind had started spinning with plans and maneuvers. Suddenly he sees that he's standing on the road, a road now overgrown with grass.

"Fine," he says, reconciling himself to seeing just whomever he manages to see. At the age of forty a person gets so fed up with bustling here and there and keeping on a schedule that finally he tells himself and his conscience (and some third presence as an observer), "Okay, this is the way I am—I'll go through life like this."

Valentina is a seamstress at a dressmaking shop (her hus-band was killed when a link broke on a construction crane; her son is in the army, her daughter in the ninth grade). Valentina felt shy about going to see him at the hotel because as a seamstress her face was too well known in the little town.

"How would it be if I go along to see the ruins of your vil-lage?"

"Uhm."

"I would really like to. And we'd spend the day there? Right? After all, we're childhood friends!"

They weren't really childhood friends. True, they had lived close to each other, but they had even been in different grades in school, so she hadn't meant anything to him grow-ing up. She was just a girl named Valya, that was all. Now this forty-something-year-old matron, stout but pretty, had turned up at the very beginning of his round of visiting kin-folks and she didn't want to part from him. They went everywhere together. If he hadn't been going to the remains of the village, he would have latched tight onto her. They had a lot to talk about, and their conversation had a special, unforced feel, because no one else *from childhood* remained here. Valentina's apartment was pleasant, but they didn't stay there long. Her ninth-grade daughter came home and put a damper on their mood.

Getting up from the table he suggested, out of inertia, that they drop by his hotel. "We'll go on reminiscing there."

"No. I can't go to the hotel—you must kidding!" Valentina hissed, then blushed. "Fine, I'll think of something." And she thought of going with him to the village.

Right then a worm started gnawing at him inside.

It was two and half hours before the train (as on the previous day, only the local train went to the village). Once they've bought the tickets, he and Valentina sit by the river and kill the two and a half hours. It's hot and tiresome. He doodles in the sand with a fallen twig, and the little worm keeps gnawing at him more and more. How did he ever agree that she should come along? He was no kid, he understood perfectly why they were going there, and he had been grateful lots of times in life to chance and coincidence, but this time he was angry. There was the heat besides. His irritation grew. "What the hell am I doing?" he thought. "What a dumb situation—a little 'business-trip' kind of affair with a woman and what surprising twist can it lead to at the end? (As if it would be impossible without *that*.) There's no question—Valentina is nice, sweet, and it's also a brush with childhood and memories, and all that sort of thing, no denying it. But for that, there is the hotel, there's a corkscrew and a bottle of wine, *room service*—city things belong in the city, but what's the point of bringing Valentina along? No, no, just not there."

He sits on a pile of broken bricks and thinks how to get rid of the girl from childhood. His designs in the sand spread wider and become more intricate. "There's time," he thinks.

Valentina sits beside him. She watches the Ural River flowing by and the cars moving across the bridge.

"Happy we're going together?"

"Yes." (He speaks with the voice of someone living, but at

the same time goes on thinking like a man from the after-life.)

"Did you know that right here by the bridge there was a underground passage—that went under the river?"

"I know." (He goes on drawing.)

"Some crazy man dug all the way through. Did you, too, hear that story as a kid?"

"Yes."

The sun is beating down. Squinting, he looks aside and finds Valentina's large knees, partially covered by her cotton print dress, right in front of his eyes. Her legs are big, with satiny skin and a light natural tan. She has a strong, succulent figure, and he swallows a lump of his sudden apostasy and refusal. He looks the other way. He had already firmly decided to wriggle away from Valentina (get out of the trip with her), and now he looks for the occasion and the words, even if it entails a little quarrel which later he will smooth over somehow with a letter from far away, with a pretty post-card.

"There also used to be a chapel here," he willingly picks up the all-but-sagging conversation (a quarrel has to emerge by itself). "It had a drawing of this weirdo trader rising into the sky. Angels were holding him up and taking him to heaven. You remember it?"

"It's all destroyed now."

"Remember the place where the chapel stood?"

"Why shouldn't I remember—we're sitting on it."

"Not really!" All but jumping, he stood up.

(Finally he found the word that he had been looking for, tapping around in a circle in his mind for so long; it explained why he didn't want to go *there* with Valentina. The word was *heresy*. Again the little worm bit at him.) He moves off to take a look around. Pieces of the fire-bricks made the old way lie heaped together, unrecognizable. They were almost level with the ground, and it was uncomfortable to sit on them. There were also the weeds of course.

"Uhm, yes," he drawls, as if articulating a deep thought. "Time—is time."

"The chapel collapsed when the ice broke on the river. The spring thaw . . . "

"I didn't know."

"They say it was from the rumbling when the ice broke up. Here by the bridge it was so strong, like an artillery barrage, and the chapel just collapsed. My neighbor was standing there at the bus stop and saw it himself. It tumbled down, just disintegrated into little pieces of brick."

Now Valentina is sitting on these little bricks with her arms clasped around her strong, round little knees.

Valentina gets up and suddenly runs toward him as if to throw herself into his arms (from happiness or what?). She hurled herself at him without warning, and he even braced his legs to be able to catch her—weight and speed combined—with proper masculine resilience, but to his surprise she yelled, "Kolya! Kolya!" and barreled right past him to a man who had just walked off the bridge. Right on the spot she explained that this is a certain Kolya Kukin, a friend of hers, a widower, a fine person and a close neighbor.

"Let's go, people! Let's go party!" Kolya Kukin beckons to them. He gives his huge shopping bag a forceful, good-natured shake, showing by the clinking that it contained all the necessities, including some bottles.

Kolya appears to be inviting them both to his place, yet not both. As a visitor he could now leave her with Kolya and himself go to the remains of the village. But it turns out that Valentina is against this idea. She emphatically wants the three of them to be together, but if she has something going with Kolya Kukin, what's the point of his presence? Two's company. Is this a whim or is she being tactful? He again firmly declines the invitation to dinner at Kukin's, but Valentina has a tight grip. "To hell with the ruins! You were there yesterday—that's enough! Let's go, we're off to party at

Kolya's!" So they got a refund for their tickets and, sure enough, were off.

They sat down to the table—two men over forty and a woman about the same age—and they take their time drinking, without making a fuss about it. As a widower Kolya has his own half of the duplex, its yard and sheds, has his own peace and quiet, and he pours drink after drink. "Well, who's ahead?" he says. Except for offering drinks, Kolya keeps quiet. He wants to outdrink him fairly: let the little Muscovite come unglued and let Valya herself choose between the two of them. The Muscovite becomes talkative as he and Valya now for the nth time rake over the past. Yurka left, Vanya went a long time ago, but what about Gelya? So outstanding, so spoiled, she got married and wound up living on a state farm and she milks cows there—who would have thought it! (Remember how her parents dressed her!) There's no pattern to the conversation, but it's increasingly confiding, and the moment is coming when the levels of intoxication will be easily felt, when the party will extend itself and there will be a mountain of drinks still ahead, and (remember how Gelya's dad planted tomatoes?) the little Muscovite feels with relief that he doesn't have to go anywhere and that they will sit and drink like this year after year until Kolya Kukin's house falls down and crumbles away, just like the little chapel.

But then against all logic, he gets up from his chair and says, "I've gotta call Moscow—I'll head back to the hotel."

Valya tries to talk him out of it. "You didn't want to call."

"Well, but still . . . I'll go to the hotel and come right back."

"You're coming back for sure?" Now it's Kolya Kukin asking him, man to man.

"I'll come," he assures Kolya with a similar wink. He walks at a fast pace, as if to speed up his fate. Now he's on his way downhill, and it's an easy walk. (When they were walking up this hill, Kolya Kukin was up ahead, they lagged behind and Valentina's dress fluttered in the wind like a banner.) Suddenly he was happy that he hadn't left his briefcase behind, with them. He goes to the train station, manages to buy a ticket, and get on the very same local train, arriving a little behind schedule, it seems. He also manages to consider that he has drunk quite a bit at Kolya's and that he mustn't sleep through his stop at the little station. From there he has to walk to the village. He's drunk and about to fall asleep, but asks a little boy sitting across from him to rouse him at the right station.

He walks quickly from the train—soon it'll be dark. Okay, it wouldn't matter if he doesn't see everything, but what's the point of going to the cemetery in the dark and not being able to make out the inscription on one cross from another. He wishes that he didn't have to rush and worry about the time, but with relief it dawns on him that he can spend the night here—it's summer! He passed through a field, then a ways beyond it turned to the right and cut across a dry gully with puny little trees. This was no short hike. Then he crossed a small meadow with tall grass, but here was a foothill, and you could see the mountain peak to the right, and to the left—the slope with the cemetery. He had made it. It was still light. He had covered several kilometers and was sweating from the fast walk, but now that the view was there, he could take his time, amble along, and drink it in.

He veers to the left, crosses the Marchenovka, then climbs up the mountain slope. It may be spreading and losing its dark green triangular form, but there it is! Better said: there *they* are. All who chose this spot for the village also lie here, even though it's been many years since all traces of the crosses on their graves have vanished. In fact, there aren't many crosses at all. There exists the quietness of a village and there's the silence of an abandoned village, but then there's the absolute silence of the cemetery of an abandoned village. This silence can be heard.

He has an hour or hour and a half of light still to spare—not a lot, so he looks at what he can and reads what he can read. About five crosses are leaning so far that they're about to fall, and the other fifteen or so have already fallen, some facing the east, some the west. The last names are the same ones—Trubnikov, Yarygin, Grushkov. They would be impossible to make out if you didn't know them in advance, but he reads them easily, whether the name lacks three letters, five, or only a syllable remains. The wood's been eaten away to dust by rain, wind, and worms. The Korols were especially unlucky—they were in the center of the cemetery, where the blackthorn was completely overrun by steppe grass and sage, where the crosses lay scattered by the wind like brushwood—one long stick and two small ones together. The fallen crosses, shrunken and thin, look small and pitiful, and only the tin marker hanging loosely on a stick or two here and there, with two of three letters still preserved, testifies to someone who can read their meaning that here lie the Korols.

The boundary between the Korols and the Grushkovs was relative—again, only someone who knew would notice. But barriers and divisions had never been here. They all lay there together. If a question arose about selecting the right spot within the tight family confines, it came only from the natural desire of a husband wanting to lie close to his wife, or she close to the children, and little Seryozha, who was brought from the city and died here, couldn't rightfully be shunted off to the side, and for that reason they placed him between his grandfather and grandmother . . . Breaking off a branch of blackthorn, the man who had come here gnawed on the thin twig and felt a wave of melancholy. He still felt the wine he had drunk, but it didn't hamper him. He wandered around, traversing a patch of sage and then coming back again to the dark green spot. He wandered this way and that, at random and according to old memory, but not to one certain place—the upper left corner of the cemetery. Managing to keep it separate within the intricate pattern of an otherwise random path, he avoided that corner. There his direct kin lay. He would go there later, and, if it were dark by then, he would see in the darkness what he needed to see.

For now he looks at them *all*. How far the chain of first names stretches and yet how short the concrete memory is! It's the rare person who can point to the grave of his great-grandfather, and certainly not everyone can even show you his grandfather's burial place. Mountain people sometimes have stone vaults that indicate such remote ancestors as to stagger the imagination, and they can take pride in this, but people of the plains never can. For that reason, as a plains-man, he was especially lucky that he knows and has at least this center of focus—never mind that it's nameless. For him *this* is dead, yet it still continues until it is finally lost with his children.

He at last goes over to his own family plot, in the upper corner of the cemetery's blackthorn triangle, where the crosses also naturally have fallen side by side and where the very earliest of the sets of years (he searched it out) coincidentally proved to be the year of the abolition of serfdom—1861–.... Who this was and when he or she died was worn away and unknown—only the year of birth was known. Among the direct kinfolk there was also one who bore only the final date—the year of death:

...–1942

only his name remained—Gleb. But logic still wanted some-thing, kept looking for something else—and found it. It was on one of the fallen crosses, or rather three little boards, which lay rotting away together. No name, no dates. On the little tin plate attached to the marker everything had been erased except for an extended dash. It looked like this:

...–...

and that was all. Eternity itself.

The sun is setting, at the end turning scarlet and even sweeping a passionate red flare across the mountain peak. The cemetery is flooded with rosy light, and the visitor knows that soon it will be dark—the light fades swiftly here, in a single moment. He catches himself and jumps to his feet (with a start and a reprimand—after all, it's no short walk to the train), but then when would he again see the sunset here and the nighttime that follows—never! This thought causes him to sit down again. Also, that bottle that he sequestered away in the ruins the day before comes to mind. It will brighten up the night ahead and keep him from freezing. After uncorking the bottle, he takes two or three bitter sips and lights a cigarette. By the time he takes his last puffs, the sun is gone.

He drinks a bit more, then a wave of intoxication hits him from within—it rolls through him to his very toes, then rushes back up again and from there to his heart. It's dark. Night. The stars have come out—this is just what *they* saw, too. Certainly this hasn't changed. He can safely say that in the darkness of the night his feelings coincide identically with *theirs:* he's found the same that they did. He leans back—the earth is warm. A new wave rolls through him: his high's building, but it's under control. He waited a second and still another, new wave followed, and obeying an urge to let go, to mark this moment (discreetly here, too), he rubs the pungent leaves of a sprig of sage in his hands and suddenly stands up and yells into the night, "H-ey-ey!" It's addressed to no one, and when his voice fades into the dead silence he drops to the ground and presses his face into the wild mint, as if turning to the earth or to the cemetery or to someone else. Finally there comes a thought, unfortified by wine, that tells him softly that he hasn't managed to avoid a certain pattern and that all of this is an ordinary occurrence and just a flirtation with eternity. And not to burst into the tunnel. But then, when he had understood, he peered still more keenly and intensely somewhere into the night, into the darkness and space, and his eyes smart from tears trickling out suddenly. "Haven't we got enough of our own burdens?" people will say. "Why should we get all worked up and heavy-hearted if some forty-year-old guy acts out such a drama on the ruins? He should be happy that he found all this and that it exists, but what about the person who doesn't have that? Where are those others, *where* do they press their faces into the wild mint?"

Orion had rolled out into the sky and all stands motionless. Grown stately and vast, the sky seems to hold no place either for people or their deeds. And the traveler feels no better, no purification. Now sober and with mind cleared, he sits for a long time. Silently he considers that it wasn't necessary to come here. There's no response.

Taking his briefcase and heading down the hill, he walks fast in the dark. The cool damp air wafting from the creek guides him. And the sound of water splashing along its rocks. It's been running there a thousand years. But length of time no longer concerns the traveler. He squeezes between the willows, crosses to the other side, and under the starry night sky sees—amazing—the old road in the darkness. He quickens his pace, it's still possible to make the train.

■ □ ■ □ ■

KLYUCHARYOV AND ALIMUSHKIN

I

ONE DAY A MAN NOTICED THAT THE LUCKIER HE BECAME IN life the worse things got for another man. He noticed it quite by chance and to his own surprise. And it bothered him. He wasn't so unfeeling as to go celebrate his own good fortune when right next door he could hear somebody crying his heart out. But that's how it turned out, or very nearly. And he couldn't redo or change anything, because not everything can be redone or changed. Then he began to get used to it.

But finally once he couldn't contain himself and went up to the other man and said, "I'm lucky, and you're unlucky . . . It's depressing me. It's interfering with my life."

The unlucky man didn't understand. And didn't believe it.

"Bull!" he answered. "Things happen and they're not connected to each other. Sure, I've had some rotten luck, but you've got nothing to do with it."

"But still, it bugs me."

"Nonsense. Don't think about it. Relax. Get on with your life."

The lucky man left and went on with his life. Still, he worried a bit, because things got worse for the other man, while he kept getting luckier. The sun was always shining his way, women smiled at him, when new bosses came along they turned out to be nice guys, and there was peace and harmony at home.

That's when he started an imaginary conversation with God.

"It's not fair," he said. "Good fortune comes to one person at somebody else's expense."

"Why is that unfair?" God asked.

"Because it's cruel."

God thought and thought again, then sighed, "There's not enough good fortune."

"Not enough?"

"Well, yeah . . . Just you try to cover up eight people with one blanket. Will any one of them get much of that blanket?"

Then God flew off. God just disappeared and didn't give an answer, or rather he gave the kind of answer that doesn't mean anything. As if he'd laughed it off.

And then the man stopped thinking about it. After all, how long can you keep thinking about the same thing? In the end it wears you down. That's essentially the whole story. But in this case the details are important . . . Klyucharyov was a scientist at a research lab, a mathematician, it seems—yes, exactly—a mathematician. His family was an ordinary one. And their apartment was the usual kind. And life, all in all, was quite average: an alternation of light and dark areas led to a certain middle ground summed up by the words "ordinary life."

Klyucharyov stood out from this "ordinariness" perhaps by his somewhat affected way of joking. On the way home from work one day he found a wallet with a tidy little sum of rubles in it lying on a path in the snow. He immediately said to himself, "Congratulations! This makes me think life's worth living."

All smiles, Klyucharyov then and there wrote the usual kind of notice. Such and such wallet found, person missing it should come claim it . . . He ended with his address at the bottom, then fastened the notice to a nail on the bulletin board at the nearest building. It was winter, and in order to write the notice and hang it up, he had to set his briefcase down on the snow. The flimsy little sheet suspended from the nail fluttered in the wind but hung on snugly. The fact that neither that day nor the next did anyone respond came as no surprise, but what was really surprising instead took place the next day, when Klycharyov's department supervisor—a constantly grumbling and obstructive administrator who had clearly never wished him well—suddenly proposed placing an article by Klyucharyov in a prestigious scientific journal. Not only that, but the supervisor didn't even hint around at coauthorship. That's why Klyucharyov, as soon as he walked in the door, told his wife, "I'm on a roll of good luck."

But Klyucharyov's wife was a quiet and modest woman who was reticent and even fearful about luck, no matter what kind it might be. She worried, for instance, when no one showed up for the wallet.

A little later that evening Klyucharyov's wife announced that she had some news. She'd forgotten about it, but just now she remembered.

"Aha!" Klyucharyov laughed. "Your friend called?"

"Yes."

"Who says I'm not quick!"

His joke was directed at a certain woman who had once worked with his wife. They had become friends, and by sheer inertia she a remained friend even now. By now it had been a long time since they had worked together, and his wife hadn't seen her for a while. But the two women called each other from time to time. They talked about their children or about shopping. Now the phone calls were becoming less frequent. In time this remnant of the women's friendship would quickly dwindle away and die, but for now it was still alive, twisted into a telephone cord.

His wife fell silent: it annoyed her that the friendship was fading to nothing and that her husband was already poking fun at their long talks on the telephone.

To soften his remark, Klyucharyov asked again, "So, what *is* the news?"

And then his wife said that Alimushkin was having some problems at work. And that in general Alimushkin was "burning out," as they say . . .

"Alimushkin?" Klyucharyov for the life of him couldn't remember who this was. He just shrugged his shoulders. Klyucharyov knew how his wife, conscientious to a fault, was always ready to take up someone's case, whoever it might be. But then he remembered the man. He'd seen him twice. "Alimushkin—is that the guy who was so bright and witty?"

"That's the one," his wife said. And she immediately added that maybe Klyucharyov could drop by to see him at home, pay a visit. Look. She'd specially jotted down his address. His wife's voice was completely serious. Even touching. He automatically took the piece of paper with the address, but couldn't suppress a snort. Women are really something! Only they could think up something like this. To go and see some guy you hardly know and say, "Hey, friend, I hear you're . . . burning out"?

"But what's the point of me going to see him? We've met all of twice in our lives."

"And I've seen him only once."

This was a weighty argument, no way around it.

"You'll agree," his wife charged ahead, "it's better and more appropriate if a man visits him."

"Better or worse—I'm not going. I don't have the time."

No quarrel occurred. The Klyucharyovs were a loving couple. His wife even admitted that maybe she was asking too much. To send him God-knows-where and for what? So, instead, they started talking about their son, a junior in high school. He was having major success in sports, at gymnastics to be exact.

Klyucharyov would have forgotten about his wife's odd request, except that the same evening there was still another telephone conversation. This time Klyucharyov called a friend named Pavel. As often happens, a phrase from one conversation crosses over and migrates to another one. The life of a phrase is short after all, and it's as if the phrase wants to live a little longer.

It turned out that instead of some word of greeting, Klyucharyov asked his friend, jokingly, "Well, how's life? You're not burning out?"

Pavel answered, "No, I'm not 'burning out.' Where'd you pick that up?"

Klyucharyov laughed and had to explain that it was a joke. He'd said it for no particular reason, just a faddish phrase. "We know, for instance, a certain Alimushkin who's burning out."

"Alimushkin?" Pavel repeated. "But we work together."

"Really?" ("Small world," he thought.)

"We work in adjoining offices." Pavel added that Alimushkin was not a bad guy, but in some kind of rut. "Something's happened to him. He just can't work at all."

"Why not?"

"Who the hell knows. He's the silent type. Frankly, I stay away from those loners."

Here they were in total agreement. Klyucharyov didn't like them either.

"Even drunks are better," Klyucharyov said. And again he remembered what Alimushkin had once been like. "But, wait, what kind of 'silent type' is he? What happened to the bright guy he used to be? Such a hotshot!"

Pavel responded with a sigh, then stated a deep, eternal truth. "Here today, gone tomorrow."

That same evening, just before bed, Klyucharyov went out for a stroll around the apartment building. He called it "airing himself out." While he followed the paths trampled down in the snow, in his head there echoed, "Here today, gone tomorrow." Suddenly, a strange thought occurred to Klyucharyov: what if he really had become lucky at Alimushkin's expense? He remembered his boss's proposal to submit an article. He remembered the incident of the wallet. And he grinned. Naturally, the thought was pretty silly— momentary and generally insignificant. The weather was frosty. There were stars overhead. He walked and looked up at the sky. How enormous! How packed full of stars! He thought how these stars had watched or even foreseen so many human successes and failures that long ago they had ceased to care. They'd grown cold in their indifference. The stars? They don't give a damn! Would they interfere and bestow success on one person and failure on another? No way.

However, Klyucharyov couldn't rid himself of that thought the next day, and this is why. He was invited to a party at Kolya Krymov's. While he was still in the hallway and taking off his coat, he heard remarks such as, "What? You haven't heard about Kolya Krymov's new love?" or like, "Kolya Krymov's new love will be coming soon," or outright mockery: "Okay, set out the glasses. But don't touch the bottle. Be patient. Any minute now Kolya Krymov's new love will appear." Jokes like these were buzzing around. The people there—men and women in their mid-thirties—all thought the best way of socializing and having fun was to tease the host. Kolya Krymov didn't object; it even flattered him. And then she came. Her last name was Alimushkin. She was a very pretty woman.

Amid the general noise and hubbub at the table, Klyucharyov asked Kolya Krymov whether he was planning to get married. They were friends. While the guests were vying with each other to serve Madame Alimushkin and some poet was inscribing his volume of verse for her, Kolya Krymov, not wanting to hide anything, answered, blushing slightly: "Yes, I'm planning to." Kolya Krymov loved neat formulations. He said that to have yet another little affair would almost be debauchery. But to get married again was like a quest . . . Just then it turned out that one of the guests had overindulged in drink, and Kolya Krymov went to find him a cab. So Klyucharyov and Madame Alimushkin began a short conversation.

They were sitting rather close with only Kolya Krymov's empty chair between them. Having nothing else to do, Klyucharyov began to talk with her. He had no special agenda in mind, no stray little thoughts.

"So, what's up with your Alimushkin?"

"Oh, to hell with him!" the beauty answered. "He keeps saying the same thing over and over: 'I'm burning out, I'm burning out . . . '"

"He just whines?"

"It's not a matter of whether he whines or not. Mainly he's silent for hours."

Madame Alimushkin was somehow brazenly beautiful. She had a certain provocative quality. Klyucharyov had never known such women. Of course, he had seen them on occasion, and they were never alone, someone was always accompanying them. Sometimes, even a man on each arm.

When their conversation lapsed, Madame Alimushkin started it up again. It came easily to her. She had a lively little tongue and a daring look. "To tell you the truth, I've stopped loving him. I'm staying at a girlfriend's. I live as I like, go to parties, and enjoy myself."

Klyucharyov saw her eyes up close. "Maybe it's when you started living at your girlfriend's and enjoying yourself that Alimushkin started burning out?" he asked.

"How can you say that!" she responded. "In fact, it's just the opposite."

And it was obvious that she was telling the truth. Their conversation ended; she started talking to the man on her left. But Klyucharyov once again remembered that thought of his. He put it this way to himself: "If my present good luck really is at Alimushkin's expense, his wife would have set her sights on me. The time was ripe. But her eyes were for Kolya Krymov. Unfortunately."

He left the party tipsy and a little confused. His mood was neither up nor down. He was thinking what he would say to his wife now: he hadn't warned her he'd be late. He took out the slip of paper with Alimushkin's address. It was close by—and . . . he headed there in order to have at least some kind of excuse. Alimushkin was asleep. It was after midnight. His coming there was peculiar, and Klyucharyov didn't know what to say.

"Were you sleeping? You know people are saying that you're burning out," he said, as if reproaching him.

Alimushkin was silent as he stood there half-asleep. Then he yawned. Klyucharyov felt awkward and dropped the casual tone.

"I hope you remember me . . . We've met before. We used to see each other at the library. And once we were at the same party."

Alimushkin nodded. "I remember." He wasn't totally awake. "Would you like some tea?" he added as if it were an afterthought.

"No, I just dropped in for a second," Klyucharyov answered with a smile. He tried to make it as friendly as possible. "Tea at this point . . . I'm up to my gills without any tea."

After that Klyucharyov left.

At home when his wife began scolding him about the alcohol on his breath, Klyucharyov got angry.

"Now wait a minute! You were the one who sent me. 'Find out this and find out that!' This Alimushkin was supposed to be my assignment. Because of him I hung out for a while at Kolya Krymov's [Klyucharyov arranged the facts pretty flexibly], and then I still had to go over to his place. It turns out the kid's alive and well. All fit and ruddy. And sleeps like a babe."

Klyucharyov was walking down the hall. He had taken a break from work for a minute or two, or maybe ten. He thought this would clear his mind, and he walked along with a light and resonant step. He was passing the doors of a big and well-furnished office, and standing right in front were Boss Number One and Boss Number Two. Number One, the director of the lab, was holding his hat in his hands. Number Two, his deputy, was in a fury about something and was trying to prove a point. But the director was chuckling.

The deputy happened to cast a glance at the person walking by. And said, "Here's Klyucharyov for you—both capable and hardworking—and a Ph.D. But you're still holding him back as a research associate."

"Maybe it's you who's holding him back," parried the director. He chuckled.

"Me?"

"Of course, you," the director grinned.

Klyucharyov stopped a pace away from them. He wasn't pushing himself on them. In fact, he was going his own way. However, to leave or walk past when you're being openly discussed or looked at was somehow awkward.

"Don't argue," he said to them quietly and calmly. "It's me—I'm keeping my own self back."

They both started smiling. They were pleased that he wasn't trying to foist himself on them.

"I'm in a hurry. One hell of a hurry!" the director said and headed for the door.

Chasing after him, the deputy said, "It's way past time to make Klyucharyov a section supervisor."

"Well, do it then," answered the director.

An hour later—and this was in no way connected with the conversation of the director and the deputy, but came entirely from *another source*—Klyucharyov learned that his article had been accepted and soon would be published. At home that evening his wife once again said, "My friend called. There's some news." And the news consisted of the fact that poor Alimushkin had been abandoned by his wife. She had left him for good. Moved out. Taking advantage of the fact that Aliumushkin was "burning out"— "*He's totally spineless, like he's always half-asleep*"—the pretty woman had traded their joint apartment for a nice studio for herself and sent the drowsy Alimushkin to live in some damp little hole somewhere. "He's living there now. And that's where he's now burning out," his wife said, and Klyucharyov couldn't help but take note that his successes and Alimushkin's failures were moving along just as before—side by side.

The next morning more news came by phone. Double trouble. Now Alimushkin got fired from his job. He mixed something up or did something wrong, and to make matters worse, he had thrown some important papers in the trash. They could have easily taken him to court, but they felt sorry for him. They simply fired him. Apparently, it wasn't so much a matter of the important papers or the contents of the trash basket. It was just that everyone was fed up with Alimushkin's sluggishness and idleness and that had been the final straw.

"How's he going to live?" asked Klyucharyov. He didn't have Alimushkin's inner life in mind. He was thinking of where he would find the money to live on.

"I don't know," answered his wife. And just because she didn't know, she asked Klyucharyov to drop in on Alimushkin again and check things out. "Stop by," she said. "Come on, it's no big deal." And she reminded him that a long ago they both had seen Alimushkin at friends' and he had been the liveliest of the bunch—so bright and witty.

Klyucharyov asked his wife, "And if he hadn't been so bright and witty, would you still feel sorry for him now—when he's got problems?"

"I don't know."

Klyucharyov immediately picked up on her wavering "don't know" and with a trace of satisfaction said, "But that's not fair, my love. You only pity the chosen few."

But as a resourceful woman she found an answer to that, too. "If he hadn't been so bright and witty, he would have been something else," she said. "For instance, quiet and sentimental, and a person like that would also deserve sympathy."

The very next morning the deputy offered him the job of section supervisor. The deputy made the offer without any conditions, but Klyucharyov turned it down—he answered that he didn't want to elbow aside the present supervisor; after all, for better or worse, they had worked together for many years. This was the truth. However, truer still was the fact that Klyucharyov didn't want to push right now—even without pushing, he felt that he was having a streak of luck and that its benefits weren't going to leave him. He had a clear, but unexplainable sense that someone from above had firmly and confidently tightened the reins and was doing the driving for Klyucharyov and, naturally, the one above knew his job and wouldn't allow any slip-up.

"Strange," the deputy asked again, "then, you don't want to be section supervisor? Are you afraid of the responsibility?"

"Yes, it's easier without a lot of pressure. I'm working hard as it is."

"We know that."

"I've got a lot of work to do, and I don't want any more right now." Klyucharyov allowed himself to answer sharply. As if to test and check his success. After all, tomorrow he could say, "Okay, now I want to. I'm ready. I agree."

He went to see Alimushkin. First, he asked, "Gee, friend, how'd you land in a dump like this? Why did you agree to give up the apartment?" Alimushkin didn't answer. He looked bad. He was sluggish, lethargic, obviously not well.

Gazing steadily at Klyucharyov, he mumbled out, "I . . . don't remember you."

Then he turned and started looking somewhere to the side. Into space.

"It makes no difference whether you remember or not. Why did you agree to live in such a hole?"

Alimushkin didn't answer. His mind was functioning slowly. He had just then managed to recognize his guest's face.

"You're . . . Klyucharyov?"

"Yes."

Meanwhile, Klyucharyov had glanced around. He had more or less known that Alimushkin, being so lethargic, hadn't bettered himself when he switched apartments, but it never dawned on him that a living soul could be thrust into such a hole. It was a tiny little room, narrow, shabby, water stains all over the walls and without furniture. Just a rusty bed, a table and one chair. It was a communal apartment, and in the next room there lived a lonely old man, and his room was just as wretched. The old man was sick, unsociable, and deaf as a post.

"He doesn't even say hello to me in the kitchen," Alimushkin related in a listless voice. "He's just silent."

"You're not too talkative either."

"Yeah . . . "

A long, painful silence ensued.

"So this is the way you live?"

He nodded, "Yes . . . "

"Do you go anywhere?"

"No, nowhere."

"Forgive me, but where's the money coming from for you to buy your groceries?"

"I've got a few rubles left. I'm using them up."

"And after that?"

A still longer pause followed. Finally, instead of an

answer, Alimushkin quietly said, "I—," and he looked at Klyucharyov as if to see whether he would laugh, "I'm playing chess . . . "

Klyucharyov didn't laugh. "That's good," he said.

"Here." Alimushkin glanced over at some little chess figures. The board was worn. The little figures were set out. "I used to play. As a kid."

"And who do you play with?"

"Not with anyone. I, uh . . . play by myself. I analyze the moves."

Klyucharyov suggested that they play, since there was nothing to talk about.

Alimushkin was a weak player. Klyucharyov played a few games with him and left. He was in a lousy mood. It would have been easier for Klyucharyov if Alimushkin had been at least an average player.

3

At Alimushkin's there was a certain moment—it had been a special moment. During one of the painful pauses Klyucharyov had thought: how did it happen that a human life had just simply gone downhill? Klyucharyov was not stupid and understood that what happens to one person can happen to another. That's just the way people are born. It's also the way people die. He asked Alimushkin, "So, how did this happen to you?"

Alimushkin was silent, he didn't quite understand what was being asked. But then he tried to understand (the effort was noticeable on his face), and he answered Klyucharyov that, no, nothing special had happened. He felt that he was burning out, and that was all.

"Did this begin when your wife left you?"

"No . . . earlier."

"Aha," Klyucharyov said, as if brightening up. "This started with your problem at work."

"No . . . "

"What started it then?"

"I don't remember."

Klyucharyov showed some impatience. With obvious annoyance he pressed Alimushkin. "But everything can't just collapse for no reason. Think back. Strain your memory. It's important to me, too. In fact, it's important to everybody—how did it start?"

Alimushkin wiped his forehead. He frowned and said, "No . . . I don't remember."

It was time to leave, because now one pause followed another. Klyucharyov peeked around, checking—yes, there was a teakettle. But there was so little tea left in the jar that he didn't even hint at having a cup. Instead he suggested they play chess. Klyucharyov easily won one game, then a second and a third. Then he rose to leave.

"See you . . . "

Alimushkin gave a vacant stare. Then he limply reached for a pen. He wanted to jot down some notes on the last game and look for his mistakes.

"It's supposed to help," he mumbled.

That's just the way he had muttered it. "It's supposed to help." And these words, emphasizing his all but total useless-ness and emptiness, rang in Klyucharyov's ears. The words were haunting. And for that reason, when Klyucharyov came home, he decided not to tell his wife the truth. That was easy, because his wife was busy with their son and daughter. She was setting the children's minds straight about some lit-tle shortcomings. Klyucharyov said as if incidentally, "I went to see Alimushkin. You know, he's not so bad off. Talkative. And absolutely calm."

"Really?"

"He's decided to take up chess seriously. All but dedicat-ing himself to it."

"Thank God. I'm happy for him."

"Soon we'll be hearing about Grandmaster Alimushkin."

It's easy to talk when you being listened to uncritically. And Klyucharyov added with some solemnity, just in case, "I respect people who start life over again."

The luck continued and now it was like a thief in reverse. An anti-thief. You close your left pocket, but it's shoved into your right one. "Take it, fine fellow, it won't be missed; go on, take it—this is your hour." At work everyone smiled at Klyucharyov and was glad to talk to him. "He's got good prospects," they said of him. Even the deputy smiled. He hemmed and hawed a bit, then said that a significant raise was in order.

"Thank you."

"I myself interceded for you. And the director supported it. For a start, we're raising your salary by one step."

"Thank you."

"We value good associates. Especially modest ones."

And the deputy added (trustingly—he wouldn't say this to everyone), "Some people elbow others aside. They intrigue. They step on people in order to get to a cushy place. I don't like those kind."

Half an hour later, Madame Alimushkin called; she somehow had found out the institute's number and immediately got Klyucharyov. Later, she said that she'd copied the number on the sly at Kolya Krymov's. For some reason it seemed to her that she had to do it surreptitiously.

She said hello and invited Klyucharyov to come over. She didn't beat around the bush; she was a pretty woman and knew it. She didn't bother to choose her words and with no embarrassment said, "On that evening . . . ," and she paused in a way that was characteristic of a contemporary woman, "I took a fancy to you."

"Now really!"

"Honest. Come over to my place, please. Today."

He went and wasn't at all dazzled by her voice and her eyes: he didn't like beautiful women; he had never known any. It was easier and more comfortable for him to live that way. He sat in an armchair and inspected the apartment—a cute little place. With great furniture.

Klyucharyov asked, "Aren't you planning to marry Kolya Krymov?"

This question really meant: "You called me to come over. Is this a whim of yours or a little secret behind Kolya Krymov's back, and in general, what kind of game is this we've started?"

But Madame Alimushkin answered simply, "No. I'm not getting married."

"Why not?"

"I don't like him. He's a nonentity. He's a good-for-nothing."

"Make him into whatever you want."

"I don't want to waste the effort. What for?"

Klyucharyov didn't start that kind of sweet and amusing conversation that would have led him in a certain direction, even though he essentially felt like going that way. Instead of taking a clear approach, Klyucharyov behaved unpredictably. All of a sudden he got angry at Madame Alimushkin and told her rudely that Kolya Krymov was even a very "good-for-something" person. And that Alimushkin, who had been abandoned, was also a "good-for-something" guy. And that she should get married, not fool around, and stop kidding herself. He kept on talking, knowing full well that what he was saying was stupid and nonsensical. Whatever the case, she was a woman, and she had the right to choose.

In his briefcase, which he hadn't opened, there were two bottles of wine. He had brought them on purpose. And he knew why. But something got into him, and now he was talking foolishly. "Get married!" he intoned over and over to her. And she was absolutely right when she said, as he was already leaving and at the door, "What a bore you are! You bore a person to death."

Klyucharyov's wife was somewhat rattled by the abundance of good fortune. She even got frightened. It took the form of a suppressed expectation that some misfortune or problem would befall them any minute. Without a word about her real reason, she decided to summon her mother—Klyucharyov's mother-in-law, that is—let her, say, come for a visit. "Let her live with us for a while. In case one of us gets sick . . . ," she said. "Or, say, something else bad happens," she let slip.

"But why should anything happen?" Klyucharyov laughed.

Klyucharyov was laughing again, he was his old jolly and joking self. He found it funny and amusing when he recalled how he had behaved and what he had said to the pretty woman who'd invited him to her house. "What a buffoon!" he would say, teasing himself. He would recall her cheeks and lips, and a sweet chill would travel down his spine.

From her own office his wife called him at his. "Are you listening? I just called my friend. It's about Alimushkin again."

"He's burning out?"

"Cut the silly stuff."

"Seems like he's taking a long time to burn out—sometimes I even think he can go on burning out forever."

"Cut it out!" And his wife started whispering into the phone. She was vaguely apprehensive of something and for that reason whispered to her husband, "Dear, be more cautious." And again whispered, "Dear, don't talk about people carelessly; dear, if only you thought about people just a bit more . . . I know you're kind and sincere, but if you would also think about people . . . " That's what she whispered. The call ended with a request—to pay another visit to poor

Alimushkin. That's the thought that occurred to her once again.

But an altogether different idea came to Klyucharyov: how to make his wife's friend shut up? How come she was constantly jabbering, how come she was always sticking her nose in?

"Hi," Klyucharyov said. After work—okay, he'd given in—he had gone to Alimushkin's, but there was no answer to his greeting. Klyucharyov entered his room—and his face fell. It showed sympathy for misfortune—Alimushkin was lying in bed. And like a white apparition, someone stood next to him: a doctor.

"Don't try to talk to him," said the doctor. "He can't talk. He's had a stroke."

The doctor explained—a stroke, or cerebral vascular trauma, not one of the strongest sorts, but still it was a stroke. "He needs quiet," the doctor said. "He needs silence. He needs special care . . . "

The the doctor snapped, "No—no! Alimushkin, you be quiet. You're not to talk. It's useless anyway."

"Has he lost his speech?" Klyucharyov asked.

"Temporarily."

"And can he move?"

"By holding on to the wall he can make it to the bathroom, but no farther."

Klyucharyov went nearer to Alimushkin, stepping carefully as he walked around the cockroaches that scurried along the floor. It was gloomy in the room. Alimushkin smiled—it was a half-smile, only on one side; his facial muscles on the other side were paralyzed. Klyucharyov winked. "Hey, what the heck hit you!" Alimushkin stretched his hand out to him, and Klyucharyov shook it.

The doctor was probably on emergency duty. He rummaged around in the papers on the table, then said, "Help me out here. Are you his friend?"

"Yes."

"Here in these papers there should be his mother's address."

"His mother's?" Klyucharyov asked in surprise.

"Somebody has to look after him."

"And the hospital—why can't he go to the hospital?"

"The hospital can't do anything special for him. Also, to transport him there in this condition would not be helpful."

Klyucharyov nodded, "I understand." Like all people, Klyucharyov assumed that you're not to argue with doctors. He asked again, "So you're calling his mother to come?"

"Not me. You." And the doctor looked at him severely, as if he also considered Klyucharyov, because of his own success, to blame for the poor man's condition. That's the way it seemed to Klyucharyov, although this was the usual look of a doctor who was harried and exhausted from his twenty-four hours of duty. "You call. 'Cause I've got to go. I've already sent an aide here twice to be with him. Now she's needed on a more critical case."

Klyucharyov nodded. He found the address and sent off a long telegram to a village in the Ryazan region. The telegraph office, fortunately, turned out to be around the corner, and there was no line at the window. Klyucharyov noted to himself with a bitter grin that—well, in this instance Alimushkin's lucky.

When Klyucharyov came back from sending the telegram, the doctor was gone. Alimushkin apologized for the trouble with a gesture of his hand: "Forgive me," it said, "that I caused you this problem." Gesturing again, he suggested, "Let's play chess," as if to say, "if you're not in a hurry." Alimushkin himself reached for the chessboard at his bedside. Klyucharyov almost didn't glance at the board. He moved the pieces around and looked at the floor, where the shiny cockroaches kept running back and forth.

Immediately after leaving Alimushkin, Klyucharyov dropped in on his wife's friend—he had sought her out. He had her address jotted down on a slip of paper: Malaya Pirogovskaya 9, Apartment 27. Klyucharyov had found this address in his wife's notebook, which he had quietly taken for a moment from her purse. Now he appeared at the woman's door and identified himself. "Hello, I'm Klyucharyov. You've been a friend of my wife's for many years, right? But, strangely enough, we've never met."

That was Klyucharyov's tone, almost friendly. Actually, he was really irritated and was about to erupt any moment. But it was just the beginning of the conversation.

"Nice to meet you," his wife's friend said. She was plump, even heavyset, and a slow-moving woman. Klyucharyov could imagine that she liked nothing better than to sit with the telephone at her ear for days on end. She had that kind of figure and that kind of bottom. To catch himself thinking like this, he knew, indicated just how worked up he was getting.

"Excuse me, but I'm going to be blunt. I'm sick and tired of the fuss you're making on the phone . . . "

"What?" She didn't understand. She was slow.

Trying to contain himself, Klyucharyov explained. "Stop calling my wife about that miserable Alimushkin. Stop getting my wife all upset and worried. Think about what you're doing. Give a break to an ordinary and relatively happy family that doesn't need to be burdened with all the misfortunes and sorrows that you may find all around you."

"But I didn't think that those calls . . . "

"But it doesn't hurt to think. This is so simple to grasp— you're not giving her any peace."

His wife's friend was silent; she was at a loss for words. Klyucharyov apologized again for being so blunt, then asked, "Do you occasionally drop in on him—on Alimushkin?"

"Very seldom."

"Well, keep on visiting him from time to time. And leave us in peace. Understand?"

His wife's friend was visibly offended. She loved to talk

on the phone and now her excuse for the calls was being taken away. She was entirely indifferent to Alimushkin, but people had to talk about something—especially women friends, and, of course, they needed to talk to each other.

Klyucharyov explained to her one more time. "You see, because of your phone calls my wife can't call her life her own. There's no pleasure in it. She wants to live life and enjoy it, but you're interfering. Even without Alimushkin we have quite enough friends and relatives who also get sick."

He had said it all. And now he waited for an answer. Finally, pursing her lips, she spoke up. "I won't call her anymore."

"Oh, no! That's not the way to do things."

"How do you think then?"

"Call her again. Put her mind at rest. Make up something pleasant. Say that Alimushkin got well, that he's fit and cheerful, that everything's fine. And that Alimushkin is leaving . . . well, say, for Madagascar on a long-term job assignment."

"To Madagascar?"

"Well, for example. To put an end, shall we say, to the topic. So that my wife won't ask you about him anymore. You get me?"

"Yes."

"I'll leave and you call her. Are you sure you follow me?"

"Yes."

"Have a nice day."

He left. Outside snow was falling. The snow was falling day and night now.

When Klyucharyov came to see Alimushkin after work the next day, he was already lying flat on his back—completely still and silent. At first sight of Klyucharyov, Alimushkin began gasping. He wanted to say something in greeting, but he couldn't even smile. "He's had another stroke. The doctor said a bad one," a soft-spoken little old woman murmured in a Ryazan accent as she hovered over Alimushkin. This was his mother; she'd come after receiving the telegram. Klyucharyov consoled her. When he gave her a small sum of money to help with expenses, she began nodding like a wooden doll and burst out crying. "May God preserve you, sir!" Klyucharyov left, and she remained sitting next to her son. Small and silent and with a white polkadot kerchief on her head, she sat as if frozen. She didn't understand how this misfortune—this sorrow—could be happening. How could her son, so strong and happy and who graduated as an engineer, now be lying flat on his back, unable to say a word?

It wasn't at all that Klyucharyov wanted to spare himself from thinking about Alimushkin. He wanted to spare his wife. She was too nervous, too sensitive. Klyucharyov decided that Alimushkin's condition was long-term and that he would visit him from time to time, but he wouldn't tell his wife.

He didn't tell her and she didn't ask him, because there was lots of noise and commotion and not much privacy now in their household: his mother-in-law had arrived! Not without ceremony of course. There was a gift for Klyucharyov's wife, one for their son, and, of course, another for their daughter. The presents may not have been expensive, but they were certainly chosen with love.

The next day, however, there was no need to be evasive with his wife. She herself said, "Forgive me for nagging you to death and making you go see him."

"Who?" Klyucharyov asked curiously.

"Alimushkin."

Then his wife joyfully informed him that her friend had called and that at last there was good news. Everything was just fine with Alimushkin. Alimushkin was cheerful and in high spirits again. Alimushkin was being witty again . . . His wife started telling him everything in detail. These details were peculiar and even in a certain way far-fetched, because the friend—the telephone addict—had tried her best. She had poured her heart into it. All her efforts and even talent went into a grand finale on the Alimushkin topic. It had to be closed—and Klyucharyov's wife retold it all. She was really pleased; she smiled and talked and talked, and Klyucharyov listened. He listened with total interest. "Where'd you say he's being sent?" he asked, even a second time.

"To Madagascar."

Then Klyucharyov started talking about something else, because the other topic was as troubling as it was sensitive. But their son, still a high school junior, had taken first place in almost all the apparatus events. On the bars he got a 9.7—an amazing score for his age group. The major coaches had taken an interest in him. Things were under way to send young Denis Klyucharyov to the national finals.

"Way to go, kid!" Klyucharyov said.

Naturally, his wife showed no signs of elation. In fact, that sense of fear so familiar to Klyucharyov flickered in her eyes, as if to say, "Now can't something else happen? The bars are dangerous." But their son interrupted and reassured her. "Never fear, Mom! Why should I fall? They'd just deduct two points from my score!" he laughed, both proud and pleased. People who saw him felt like saying, "That's Klyucharyov—Klyucharyov's son!"

4

On Friday Klyucharyov gave his okay to the deputy. His agreement was vague, but in essence it really meant yes. And now the deputy led Klyucharyov from room to room. "Well, how do your future colleagues look to you? Like them?"

"I like them," answered Klyucharyov. By combining two laboratories and adding some other, unassigned staff, a new section was being formed at the institute. It was going to be a brand-new unit, and Klyucharyov wouldn't have to kick or step over anyone to become a supervisor.

He was thinking exactly about that fact. But the deputy

was going on and on about what a great lab section it would be. "Powerful. On the cutting edge. And, we must presume, a friendly place. You hear me, Klyucharyov?"

"How could I not hear when you're saying it for the third time?" Klyucharyov replied.

"I'll even say it a hundred times," the deputy laughed. "I'm trying to tempt you."

"I'm already tempted."

"And I'm tempting you some more, so you won't back out."

"You think I can handle it?"

"Come on. Cut it out!"

Continuing to talk as he walked through the lab, shaking hands with one of the technicians and winking good-naturedly, as if to say, "Keep working . . . keep at it, I won't distract you." He nodded to a couple of the staff and shook hands with others. He and Klyucharyov were walking past the work tables and talking quietly.

"Choose yourself a nice secretary. See those three girls over there?"

"Yes."

"Notice the little redhead."

"The prim-faced one?"

"Yes. She's a smart little thing. And really does her best. All your papers and files will be in perfect order."

"Thanks."

They talked quietly. Then they stepped out in the hall.

"And now over to Lab Six," said the deputy.

On the way there Klyucharyov stopped for a minute and lit a cigarette. He had a certain thing to say and he thought it was better to say it right away. Better sooner than later.

"A small query . . . ," he began. "When someone moves a person up, then later this someone can hang a rope around that person's neck. It won't work with me."

The deputy laughed. "That's excellent. Be independent."

"I'm not joking."

The deputy patted him on the shoulder. "Don't worry in advance. Nobody's going to put a rope around your neck. In any case, not me."

The deputy was a happy and jolly sort of person, and Klyucharyov was a similar type. Such people will always find common ground. Klyucharyov simply thought that at this moment he needed to be on guard.

When Klyucharyov returned home, everyone there already knew everything. Both in the hallway and throughout the apartment you could almost physically feel the mood of a small family celebration. Kolya Krymov had already called and offered his congratulations. Pavel had phoned with his best wishes. It turned out that both Kolya and Pavel and other friends were about to descend on them to celebrate. His mother-in-law was beaming. She was pleased that the Klyucharyovs were on their way up.

"I'm going to fix you food for the gods today!" his mother-in-law announced. And sure enough, she trotted off to Nature's Gifts meat market and brought back an impressive leg of venison. Roasted and dripping with juices, the crimson-red leg on an enormous white platter was bound to be totally irresistible. The leg roasted in the oven for some forty minutes. Before that it was basted with cream, so that when the deer blood trickled out from the heat, it would form a pink crust that would positively enflame the appetite.

The leg was done! Klyucharyov went to buy some wine. Just when he came back, Madame Alimushkin called.

His mother-in-law didn't approve. Klyucharyov had gone to the phone when she thought he should be polishing the floor or at least opening the bottles. That, after all, was the primary job for the man of the house.

On the phone Madame Alimushkin said, "I want to thank you." And she explained exactly what she was thanking him for: it was the advice not to squander herself and to get married. She really had come to her senses and had already found a nice man, a professor and not even very old. He's very kind. And loves her very much . . . She spoke with barely discernible irony, and Klyucharyov understood which way the wind was blowing. It wasn't hard to grasp.

"I'm happy for you," he said.

Just then his mother-in-law said, "Why's he chattering away on the phone!"

And his wife explained, "He has things to take care of, Momma."

"I know what 'things.'"

"Momma!"

Klyucharyov continued his conversation. "I'm happy for you," he said with a laugh. "It turns out I'm not needed anymore."

"Well, why not?" A tugging note crept into the pretty woman's voice. "You gave me a thump on the head, and that was right. I appreciate it. I've even changed my attitude. But still in the future . . . I may need some more advice."

"From me?"

His mother-in-law said, "He thinks I don't guess what they're talking about."

"Momma, don't be suspicious."

"And don't you defend him. What's he chattering on for? Better if he polished the floor."

"Momma!"

Madame Alimushkin said, "I would like very much to have a wise friend. And there's nothing special about it—just a wise and faithful friend, okay?"

Klyucharyov smiled. "Sure, sure, a wise and faithful friend. Just like in the movies."

"Is he calling himself wise?"

"Momma!"

"I'm not planning to press you to come over in the next few days, but still you might come see me sometime, not necessarily in the evening, even during the week, even if once a month, okay? And sometimes—not often—I'll call you. And ask you for wise advice, may I?"

"Give me a call," Klyucharyov said.

"Let her call . . . Just let her. Once I hear that sweet little voice, she'll get a dose of medicine from me."

"Momma! You ought to be ashamed! Why are you so sure it's a woman calling him?"

"And why should I think it's a man?"

The guests assembled. Some alone, some as couples, they came with bottles in their briefcases and all sorts of kind words in their hearts. Klyucharyov's wife led everyone to the table, seated them, and smiled. She had stopped being afraid of the good fortune that had come tumbling down on them, and it no longer seemed to her that the gods would go into a fury, that something bad would happen. She'd gotten used to it.

Klyucharyov rightly detected the change in her face. And for that reason, when he was asked to say something, while the guests all around were loudly congratulating him, he started by teasing his wife.

"Success is a good thing," he said and raised his glass high, "but the person who's afraid of it gets used to it the fastest."

He glanced in his wife's direction. Everybody laughed.

"And good for her that she's getting used to it!" someone shouted out.

"I won't argue. Good for her . . . But she's already used to it, now it won't be enough. Soon she'll want more—new successes. That's the way a person's made . . . "

"I won't," his wife said with laughter. "I won't want more. I'm too afraid."

Everyone laughed and shouted, "Yes, you will! You will! You'll want more success!" And when Klyucharyov proposed a toast, they started clinking glasses. His toast went like this: "May success come to everyone!" Then they ate and drank, and at the end of the evening Klyucharyov's wife started showing pictures of Denis doing his most difficult gymnastic exercises. The pictures were passed from hand to hand, and they were indeed impressive. One of them captured Denis for all eternity, as he reached the peak of his highest vault on the bars. Their son frozen on his outstretched arms, his slender legs—a gymnast's legs—totally vertical, pointing skyward. Klyucharyov's wife showed the picture for the first time. Before she had thought she would be tempting fate to show such photos.

The guests dispersed. They were pleased with the hosts, and the hosts were pleased with them. Klyucharyov's wife and mother-in-law cleared the dishes away. His mother-in-law had drunk a drop too much and was humming.

Klyucharyov and his wife were lying in bed and gradually drifting off to sleep, they talked about all kinds of unimportant things. First he yawned, then she yawned. The children were asleep. It was past midnight.

"So is she leaving?" Klyucharyov asked about his mother-in-law and yawned again.

"She's already bought her ticket."

"By plane?"

"Why do you always want Momma to fly?"

"Um . . . comfort. Speed."

They were silent. Then Klyucharyov said that tomorrow he'd go to the library, pick up some books, then maybe look in on Alimushkin. He wondered how he was doing. "I'll drop in on him tomorrow. I'll check."

"You can stop going to see Alimushkin," his wife said. "My friend called. He left for Madagascar."

"He already left?"

"Yes."

"When?"

"She said he took off at ten o'clock this morning. She said, 'Tell your husband that Alimushkin has left. And that his mother saw him off.'"

Klyucharyov was silent. Then he suddenly felt like having a smoke and went out to the kitchen. His wife was already asleep.

■ □ ■ □ ■

THE PRISONER
FROM THE CAUCASUS

I

THE SOLDIERS, MORE LIKELY THAN NOT, DIDN'T KNOW THAT *beauty will save the world,** but on the whole both of them knew what beauty is. In the mountains they felt it (a beauty of place) all too well. It frightened them. A stream leaped out suddenly from a mountain gorge. An open meadow, shining with blinding yellow hues in the sun, put them even more on guard. Rubakhin, the more experienced, walked ahead.

Where had the mountains suddenly gone? This space, bathed in sunlight, reminded Rubakhin of a happy childhood (which he didn't have). A grove of "southern" trees (he didn't know their name) stood in stately formation above the grass. But what moved the plainsman in him most of all was the tall grass itself, stirring in a gentle breeze.

"Hold on, Vov. Don't rush," Rubakhin warned softly.

To be in an unfamiliar open place is the same as being between crosshairs. And before venturing out of the thick brush, the rifleman Vovka raises up his carbine and with particular deliberation aims it from left to right, using the optical sights like binoculars. He holds his breath and surveys the space so flooded with sunlight. Beside a knoll he notices a little transistor radio.

---

* Dostoevsky, *Diary of a Writer.*

"Aha!" the rifleman Vovka exclaims in a whisper. (The knoll was dry. The little radio had flashed like glass in the sunlight.)

In quick, short bounds the two soldiers in camouflage fatigue shirts make it to a ditch, dug out halfway for a gas line (and forgotten long ago)—then to the knoll, red with fall colors. They turned the little radio over in their hands: they immediately recognized it by its shape. When Private Boyarkov would get drunk he liked to go off by himself and lie down somewhere, cuddling this little transistor in his hands. Spreading through the clumps of tall grass, they go looking for the body. Then, nearby, they come across it. Boyarkov's body is propped up by two rocks. He'd met his death. (Shot point blank. He hadn't even managed to wipe his drunken eyes, it seemed. Cheeks all hollow. In the unit they had decided that he had deserted.) No kind of ID. It has to be reported. But why didn't the guerrillas take the transistor? Because it's evidence. No. Because it's getting too old and makes a lot of static. Not a hot item. The irreversibility of what occurred (death is one of those clear-cut cases) pushes things ahead, urges you on, like it or not: it makes both soldiers extremely edgy. Using some flat rocks for shovels, they quickly and energetically bury the dead man. Then, when they have just as quickly built a mound of dirt over him (a conspicuously artificial knoll), the soldiers move on.

And again—at the very exit from the gorge—more tall grass. Not the least burned. Gently swaying. And in the sky birds are singing so joyfully (above the trees, above both soldiers). In this sense it's possible that beauty will in fact save the world. It turns up from time to time, like a sign. Not letting a person wander off the path. (Stepping along nearby. Keeping a lookout.) By making you alert, beauty makes you remember.

But this time the open, sunny spot turns out to be familiar and safe. The mountains give way. Ahead there's a smooth path, a bit farther on, a dusty fork well worn by vehicles, and right over there—the army unit. The soldiers automatically speed up their pace.

Lieutenant Colonel Gurov is not at the unit though; he's at home. They have to go there. Without taking a moment's break, the soldiers trudge over to where the colonel lives. He's omnipotent not just in this place, but even in all the adjacent (beautiful and just as sunny) places of the earth. He lives with his wife in a nice country house with a veranda encircled by a grape arbor, a spot for relaxing; this house is well tended. It's a hot time of day—noon. Gurov and his guest Alibekov are on the open veranda; feeling languid after dinner, they doze in the wicker chairs while waiting for their tea. Stumbling and with considerable timidity, Rubakhin gives the report. Gurov gazes sleepily at the two of them, covered with dust (they had come to him without being called, and he didn't know their faces at all, which also was not in their favor); suddenly Gurov becomes more animated; raising his voice sharply, he barks out that no matter who it is there'll be no assistance given: the very idea of helping those devils! It's laughable for him to hear that he's being asked to send his men somewhere to rescue trucks that got stuck in a canyon out of the drivers' own stupidity.

What's more—he won't even permit them to return. Infuriated, he orders both soldiers to get busy with the sand: let them do some honest work—they can help him in the yard. *Ab-out face!* They are to spread the mountain of sand standing by the driveway. It's to be spread along all the walkways!—to the house and the garden—there's mud everywhere, not a frigging place to set your foot down! The colonel's wife, like all practical managers everywhere, was glad to get some free help from the soldiers. Anna Fyodorovna—with rolled-up sleeves and in dirty, torn men's shoes and shouting happily—appears immediately in the vegetable garden: come on, let them also help her with weeding the beds!

The soldiers move the sand in wheelbarrows. They shovel it out and spread it along the paths. The day's hot. But the sand, taken no doubt from the creek, is moist.

Vovka propped up the slain rifleman's transistor in the sand and found the kind of music with a beat that kept him going. (But not loud—just for his own pleasure. Not to bother Gurov and Alibekov, still talking on the veranda. Judging from the slow words drifting over, Alibekov was striking a bargain for weapons—an important matter.)

The transistor on the sandy knoll once again reminded Rubakhin what a beautiful place Boyarkov had picked to die in. The dumb little drunk had been afraid to sleep in the woods, so he went out in the meadow. Even up on a little hill. When the guerrillas rushed in, Boyarkov pushed his radio aside (his faithful pal) so that it slid off the knoll and into the grass. He was afraid they would take it from him—as if to say, "Me—okay, but the radio—no way!" No, that's unlikely! He was drunk when he fell asleep, and the radio simply slipped out of his hands and slid, little by little, down the slope.

They killed him point-blank. Young guys. The kind who want to kill their first man as soon as possible so they can develop a taste for it. Even one who's asleep. The radio stood now on a pile of sand, and Rubakhin saw the red knoll, with two tenacious bushes on the northern slope, shining in the sunlight. The beauty of the place was striking, and Rubakhin—in his memory—holds on to the slope (stores it, more and more, inside himself), the place where Boyarkov fell asleep, that knoll, the grass, the golden branches of the brush, and all combining to make one more experience in survival, which is totally irreplaceable. The beauty is constant in its attempt at saving. It calls out to the person in his memory. It reminds him.

At first they pushed the wheelbarrows through the sticky mud, then they figured out a better way—they stretched boards out along the paths. Vovka neatly rolls his wheelbarrow ahead; behind him, loaded with a mountain of sand, Rubakhin pushes his huge barrow. He's stripped his shirt off, his powerful body, moist with sweat, glistening in the sun.

2

"I'll give ten Kalashnikovs. I'll give five crates of cartridges. Did you hear, Alibek? Not three, but five crates."

"I heard you."

"But with the agreement that we get the provisions by the first . . . "

"Petrovich, I take a nap after dinner. As far as I know, so do you. Did Anna Fyodorovna forget to bring our tea?"

"She didn't forget. Don't worry about the tea."

"Why shouldn't I worry!" the guest laughs. "Tea isn't the same thing as war; tea gets cold."

Gurov and Alibekov gradually renew their endless conversation. But the languor of their words (like the laziness of their argument) is deceptive: Alibekov had come for arms, and Gurov, his officers, and soldiers badly need provisions, food. The currency of exchange, of course, is arms; sometimes, gasoline.

"Grub by the first of the month. And it has to be without these idiotic ambushes in the mountains. Wine is not a necessity. But at least some quantity of vodka."

"There's no vodka"

"Look for it, Alibek, look for it. I'll look for some cartridges for you!"

The colonel calls his wife: how's the tea coming? Oh, what superb, strong tea is on its way! "Anya, what's the problem? You yelled from the garden that you'd already made it!"

In anticipation of the tea, both, in a state of after-dinner torpor, lazily light cigarettes. The smoke with similar laziness floats off the cool veranda onto the grape arbor and swirls out toward the garden.

Signaling to Rubakhin as if to say, "I'll try to get some booze (now we're stuck here)," the rifleman moves step by step out to the wattle fence. (Vovka was full of sly signals and gestures.) A young woman with a baby is standing beyond the fence, and Vovka the rifleman immediately exchanges winks with her. In a flash he jumps over the fence and starts up a conversation. Way to go! And Rubakhin pushes the wheelbarrow full of sand back and forth. To each his own. Vovka is one of those fast-moving soldiers who can't tolerate long, drawn-out jobs. (Or any other kind of work either.)

And just look: they've hit it off! Amazing how this young married woman plays up to him, as if she were just waiting for a soldier who would say some affectionate word to her. But mind you, Vovka is likable, smiles easily, and when he hangs back anywhere for an extra second, he finds a pal.

Vovka gives her a hug; she slaps his hands. The usual thing. They're in plain sight, and Vovka understands that he needs to draw her into some hut, out of sight. He tries to talk her into it, tries to pull her forcibly by the hand. The young woman is resistant. "And so, there's just no place!" she laughs. But with each step they both head in the direction of a hut whose door has been left ajar because of the heat. And soon they are there. But a little boy goes on playing with a cat in front of the door.

Meanwhile, Rubakhin struggles with his loads of sand. In spots where he can't push through, he takes the boards from their previous places and lays them out again, then guides the wheel carefully along them as he balances the weight of the sand.

Colonel Gurov continues his unhurried haggling with Alibekov; his wife (she had washed her hands and put on a pretty blouse) serves them tea, each with his own two delicate little teapots, in accordance with eastern custom.

"She brews a fine tea, she has the knack!" Alibekov praises her.

Gurov: "And why are you being so stubborn, Alibek! If you really look at it, you yourself are a prisoner. So make sure you don't forget where you are. You're sitting in my house."

"How come you say *yours?*"

"Well, for one thing—the valleys are ours."

Alibekov laughs. "You're kidding, Petrovich. I'm no prisoner—it's you who's the prisoner!" He laughs, pointing out at Rubakhin, rolling his wheelbarrow along the path with a grunt. "He's a prisoner. You're a prisoner. And in general every one of your soldiers is a prisoner!"

He laughs again. "I'm no prisoner at all."

He goes for his point another time. "Twelve Kalashes. And seven crates of cartridges."

This time Gurov laughs. "Twelve, ha! What kind of figure is that—twelve? Where do you get that kind of figure? Ten is what I can understand—numbers that are easy to remember. Okay, ten barrels!"

"Twelve.

"Ten . . . "

Alibekov sighs gleefully. "What an evening there'll be tonight! Whew!"

"Evening's a long time off."

They slowly drink their tea. It's the unhurried conversation of two people who have known and respected each other for a long time. (Rubakhin rolls his wheelbarrow on another run. He tilts it. Some sand sifts out. Spreading the sand out with a shovel, he evens the ground.)

"Petrovich, you know what the old men are saying? We've got wise old men in the little towns and *auls.*"*

"What're they saying?"

"They say it's time to make a march on Europe. Time to go there again."

"Get serious, Alibek. Eur-ope!"

"And so? Europe's there. The old men say that it's not that far. The old men are unhappy. The old men say that we go

---

* *Aul*—mountain village, Turkic.

wherever the Russians go, but what are we shooting at each other for?"

"You go ask your *kunaks**—what's the point of it?" Gurov shouts angrily.

"Oh-oh-oh, you're offended. *We drink tea, we warm our spirits.*"†

They're silent for a while. Alibekov starts to discuss matters again as he unhurriedly pours his tea from the pot to the cup. "No, it's not that far away. From time to time it's necessary to go into Europe. The old men say that then peace will come at once. Life will become itself again."

"Things will straighten out. Hold on!"

"The tea is excellent. Ah, Anna Fyodorovna, make us some more. Please!

Gurov sighs. "True, it'll be a fantastic evening tonight. You're right."

"I'm always right, Petrovich. Okay, ten Kalashes, I agree. But seven crates of cartridges . . . "

"Your own way again. Where do you get these figures— there's no such thing as the number seven!"

The hostess carries the dinner leftovers (in two white pots) to feed the soldiers who had come. Rubakhin lets out a lively whoop: yes! yes! And what soldier would refuse?

"But where's the second soldier?" she asks.

At this point Rubakhin, stuttering for words, is forced into a brazen lie: "I think his stomach is messed up." Thinking a second, he adds with a little more conviction, "Poor guy's freaking out."

"Maybe he gorged himself on fresh vegetables and apples," the colonel's wife suggests gently.

The fresh vegetable soup was delicious; it had chopped egg and pieces of sausage. Rubakhin readily bent over the first pot. At the same time he loudly knocked his spoon against the top of the pot, making it ring. A signal.

---

* *Kunak*—trusted friend, Turkic.

† In the style of a Caucasian saying.

Vovka the rifleman hears (and, of course, understands) the sound of a spoon ringing against a pot. But he doesn't care about eating. The young woman also hears (and understands) the sounds drifting from the yard—a cat meowing in distress and the immediate cry of a little boy who's just been scratched. "Ma-ama!" Evidently he'd been pestering the cat. But at this moment the woman was occupied by feelings: longing for affection and not wanting to let the opportunity escape, she's carried away and embraces the rifleman. About him, what's there to say? A soldier's a soldier. And then, once again, comes the child's capricious cry, "Ma-ama!"

Dashing out of bed the woman sticks her head out the door, hushes the little boy, and shuts the door firmly. Stamping barefoot across the floor, she returns to the soldier and it's as if she's on fire again. "Wow, you're hot! Oh, you put out!" Vovka is enraptured, but she covers his mouth. "Shhh . . . "

In a whisper Vovka puts forth a simple, soldierly command: he asks the young woman to walk to the village store and buy him a bottle of cheap local sweet wine; they won't sell it to a soldier in uniform, but she can do it like a charm . . .

He even shares a major concern with her: they don't need just a bottle now—they need a crate of wine.

"What for?"

"Payment. They've closed the road on us."

"But if it's wine you need, why did you come to the colonel's?"

"Crazy, so we came."

The young woman starts crying suddenly and tells him that recently she lost her way somewhere and got raped. Vovka the rifleman lets out a whistle of surprise: man, it's that bad! With sympathy (and curiosity), he asks how many of them were there? Four of them, she sobs, wiping her eyes with a corner of the sheet. He would like to question her a little more. She doesn't feel like talking. She buries her head in his chest, her mouth covered by his body: she'd like some words of solace, just simple feelings.

They talk some: yes, of course, she'll buy him a bottle of wine, but only on the condition that the rifleman will go with her to the store. She will hand the bottle over to him as soon she buys it. She can't go home with a bottle, not after what happened to her—people know, what will they think . . .

There was also something to eat in the second pot: kasha and a piece of canned meat; Rubakhin stuffs it all down. He eats slowly, not greedily, then washes it down with a couple of mugs of cold water. The water gives him a little chill, and he puts on his fatigue shirt.

"Let's break for a bit," he says to himself and walks out to the fence.

He drops down and starts to doze off. The hushed words of an agreement drift from an open window of the little neighboring house.

Vovka: "I'll buy you a present. A pretty scarf. Or I'll look for a shawl for you."

She: "You'll leave." She started to cry.

Vovka: "So I'll send it if I do. You don't have to doubt!"

For a long while Vovka begged her to bend over while standing. Vovka wasn't very tall (he never tried to disguise this and gladly told the other soldiers), but he loved to grab a hefty woman from behind. Couldn't she understand? It's so nice when the woman is big . . . She pushed him away, refused him. To their long, heated whispering (the words became soon indistinguishable) Rubakhin drifted off to sleep.

Outside the store, as soon as she hands him the bottle of wine, Vovka sticks it in one of the deep, sturdy pockets of his army pants and—presto, in a run—makes off to Rubakhin, whom he had deserted. The young woman had helped him so much and she shouts after him. Keeping her voice down with a certain caution on the street, she yells after him in reproach, but Vovka waves her off. He's no longer concerned with her—that's it, that's it, time to go! He runs down the narrow street. He takes a shortcut to Colonel Gurov's house and runs between the fences. He's got some news (and what news!). While keeping an eye out (awaiting his bottle), the rifleman had stood beside the grimy little store and overheard it from some soldiers walking by.

He leaps over the fence, but finds Rubakhin asleep and gives him a shove.

"Rubakh, listen! It's true—Lieutenant Savkin's going into the woods on a raid."

"Huh?" Rubakhin looks at him with sleepy eyes.

Vovka spews the words out. He propels them. "They're heading for a raid—to capture weapons. We should go with them. We'll grab some *churka** or other —that would be great! You yourself said . . . "

Rubakhin is awake by now. Yes, he understood. Yes. Matter of fact, it would be. Ye-ah, more than likely we'd have some luck there—gotta go. The soldiers very quietly make their way out of the colonel's place. They carefully gather their haversacks and weapons left by the well. They climb over the wattle fence and go out someone else's gate, so that the two men on the veranda won't see them and won't call out.

They didn't see them; they didn't call. They're still sitting there.

It's hot. Quiet. And Alibekov very softly croons in a clear voice:

All's gone qui-et here till the mo-orn . . . †

Silence.

"People don't change, Alibek."

"Don't change, you think?"

"Just get older."

"Ha! Like the two of us . . . " Alibekov pours a thin

---

* *Churka*—Russian pejorative slang for person from Caucasus or Central Asia, from *churek*, flat bread.

† Refrain from popular, semi-official Russian song "Evenings Near Moscow" by Vasily Solovyov-Sedoy.

stream of tea into his cup. He doesn't feel like haggling any-more. It's sad. Besides, he's already said all the words, and the right words (by their own unhurried logic) will make their way to his own old friend Gurov. They don't have to be spo-ken aloud.

"You know good tea has completely disappeared."

"Let it."

"Tea's going up in price. Food's going up. But time doesn't cha-ange." Alibekov draws the words out.

The hostess at that very moment brings out two more fresh pots of tea. Tea—that's true. The price is rising. *But whether the times change or not, you, brother, will supply us with food . . . ,* Gurov thinks, and he also doesn't pronounce his words aloud.

Gurov knows that Alibekov is a little smarter, a little more cunning than himself. For that reason he, Gurov, has a few solid ideas, thought through to such pure clarity over long years that they're not even thoughts anymore, but parts of his own body, like arms and legs.

Earlier (in those old days), during quartermaster failures or simply delays with the soldiers' food supplies, Gurov would immediately put on his dress coat and pin his little decoration and medals on his chest. Then in a GAZ-69 jeep (stirring up such dust, such a breeze!) he would speed along the winding mountain roads to the main town of the region, roll up to the familiar big building with columns, and stride in at full pace (not glancing at the visitors and petitioners worn out from waiting) straight into the headquarters. And if it wasn't at the Regional Party Headquarters, then it was at the Executive Office. Gurov knew how to get what he want-ed. Occasionally he himself drove to the base and gave the bribe, sometimes even sweetening it by presenting to the nec-essary person a beautiful pistol with his name engraved on it. ("May come in handy: East is East!" He never at all thought that these words, said in jest, would come to be true.) But what does a mere pistol amount to now? A pure frill! Now ten gun barrels is not enough—give me twelve. He, Gurov, has to feed his men. With age, changes come harder for a person, but in exchange, you become more understanding of human weaknesses. It even balances out. In the same way he also has to feed himself. Life continues, and Lieutenant Colonel Gurov helps it on its way: that's his whole answer. As a trader in arms he doesn't think about the consequences. What's his role here? Life itself shifted over to a place where any kind of tradeoff is possible (change whatever into whatever—you name it), and Gurov, too, changed. Life itself shifted over to war (and what a dumb war—neither war nor peace!), and Gurov naturally went to war. He went to war, but he didn't shoot. (Only from time to time, on orders, he took arms away. Or, finally, he did shoot on another order, from above.) He'll cope with this period, too; he'll hit it off now. But . . . but, of course, he's down about it. He misses those old times when he rolled up in his own little Gazik jeep, when he strode into the main office and could let himself yell and cuss to his heart's content, then later, agreeing condescendingly to talk terms, he would spread out in a leather armchair and smoke with the boss of the Regional Committee, all palsy-walsy. Let the petitioners wait outside the office door. Once, he didn't find the boss either at his office or at home. However, he found his wife in. (He had driven over to his house.) There, too, he wasn't refused. To the fine-looking Major Gurov, who was just beginning to gray, she gave everything that a woman who has been left alone for an entire week in summer and is bored can give. Everything she could. Everything and even more, as Gurov gave it a thought (having in mind the keys to the huge refrigerated Warehouse No. 2, their regional packing plant, where freshly smoked meat was stored).

"Alibek, I just remembered. Could you get some smoked meat?"

The weapons seizure (an encirclement called "horse shoe-ing" ever since General Yermolov's time)* had succeeded as an operation in surrounding the guerrillas except for the fact that the circle around them couldn't quite be closed. Only one way out of it was left. Racing along this route, the guerrillas spread apart into a broken chain, so that in an ambush, to take any one of them—either from the right or the left—and drag them into the brush (or in a jump knock them off the trail into a gorge and there disarm them) was not the easiest thing in the world, but it was possible. Of course, all this was while frequent overhead shelling went on, scaring and causing them to try to get away.

Both soldiers had sneaked into the group of men selected to undertake this "disarmament" raid. Vovka, however, got caught and sent away at once. First Lieutenant Savkin relied only on his own men. The lieutenant glanced over Rubakhin's powerful build, but he didn't make a fuss about him, didn't toss him out, and the wheezy command "Two steps forward!" was not consistent; more than likely, the lieutenant simply didn't notice. Rubakhin stood with the group of the strongest and toughest soldiers; he blended in with them.

But as soon as the shelling started, Rubakhin rushed and got into the ambush; he had a smoke behind some bushes with a certain rifleman named Gesha. They were soldiers who had seen long hitches of duty and now recalled others who had gotten discharged. No, they didn't envy them. Why the heck envy them? Who knows where you're better off . . .

"They're running like hell," Gesha said without glancing at the shadows flashing by in the bushes.

The guerrillas ran in twos and threes, hurriedly and loud-ly crashing through the ancient trail overgrown with under-

---

* A. P. Yermolov (1777–1861), Russian army commander in the Caucasus, 1816–1827.

brush. But one of the single evaders had already been hit. A shriek. The sound of a tussle . . . and silence. (*Get him?* Gesha with a look questioned Rubakhin, and he answered with a nod, *Got him.*) And once again there arose the sounds of men crashing through bushes. They were close. They just barely knew how to get some shots off (also, to kill, of course), but to run through the underbrush with weapons in their hands, with cartridge belts slung around their necks and while under fire, of course, was tough. Scared, stumbling upon the firing from ambushes, the guerrillas themselves headed up the trail, which seemed to grow narrower at every step and would lead them into the mountains.

"Hey, that one'll be mine, okay?" Rubakhin said, rising up and quickening his pace to close the gap.

"Good luck!" Gesha quickly finished his cigarette.

It turned out that it wasn't just one, but two men running past; once he'd jumped out from the bushes, Rubakhin couldn't possibly let them go. Rubakhin made a poor start. He couldn't immediately get all his muscles activated and up to speed, but once he was under way neither a thick bush in his path nor slippery ground underfoot mattered—he flew.

He sped on, several yards behind one of the men. But the first one (the guerrilla running up ahead) ran faster and was getting away. The second one (he was close now) gave Rubakhin no cause for alarm; he saw the automatic bouncing around his neck, but the shells were empty (or did the fighter have trouble shooting while on the run?). The first was more dangerous, he didn't have an automatic, and that meant that he had a pistol.

Rubakhin moved faster. He heard someone running behind him—uh-huh, so Geshka was covering. Two on two . . .

When he caught up with the second one, he neither grabbed nor tackled him (while you're dealing with him, when he's brought down, the first one will escape for sure). With a strong punch to the left, he knocked him into a ravine, into some brittle bushes, and shouted to Gesha, "One's in the ditch! Get him!" and took off after the first one, who had long hair.

Rubakhin ran at top speed, but the other man was also a runner. Rubakhin would barely begin to catch him when he, too, would pick up speed. Now they were going at the same pace, eight to ten yards apart. From up ahead the runner turned around, raised his pistol, and fired: Rubakhin saw that he was quite young. He shot again. (And he lost speed. If he hadn't fired, he would have gotten away.)

He fired over his left shoulder and the bullets were way off mark, so Rubakhin didn't duck every time he lifted his arm to shoot. But he didn't fire off all his shells, the cunning bastard. He was about to get away. Rubakhin immediately understood what he had to do. Without hesitating a moment, he flung his rifle under the runner's feet. That, of course, was enough.

The man cried out in pain, jerked, and started to collapse; Rubakhin leaped on him, trampled him, and with his right hand grabbed the wrist holding the pistol. The pistol was gone. He had dropped it when he fell—some warrior! Rubakhin led him off, twisting his arms painfully behind his back. His prisoner groaned and went limp. Rubakhin, still all flushed, took a strap from his pocket, tied up the prisoner's hands, sat him down by a tree, and shoved the slim figure up against the trunk—sit there! And only then did he finally get up from the ground and walk along the trail, recovering his breath and hunting in the grass, with sharp eyes again, both for his own rifle and for the pistol the fugitive had tossed aside.

Again a tramping of feet—Rubakhin skipped off the trail to the scraggly oak where the man he had caught sat. "Quiet!" Rubakhin ordered him. In an instant several lucky and fleet-footed guerrillas dashed past. Rubakhin didn't interfere. He had done his job.

He glanced at his captive: the face startled him. First by its youth, however, such boys, sixteen or seventeen years old, turned up fairly often among the fighters. The even features, the tender skin. The face, native to the Caucasus, struck him in some other way, but what was it? He didn't quite get it.

"Let's go," Rubakhin said, helping him (his arms twisted behind his back) get up.

As they walked, he warned him. "And don't run away. Don't even think about it. I won't shoot. But I'll beat the daylights out of you, understand?"

The young captive was limping. The rifle Rubakhin had tossed had wounded his leg. Or was he faking it? Someone who's caught usually tries to create sympathy for himself. He limps. Or coughs heavily.

4

There were a lot of captives—twenty-two men, and maybe that's why Rubakhin managed to hold on to his own prisoner without a problem. "This one's mine!" he repeated, keeping his hand on the prisoner's shoulder amid the general noise and hubbub during the final stage of trying to get the captives in formation to take them back to the unit. The tension just wouldn't dissipate. The prisoners bunched up together, afraid that now they would be split up. They hung on to each other, yelling back and forth in their own language. Several didn't even have their hands tied.

"Why is he yours? Look how many there are—they're all ours!"

But Rubakhin shook his head: "They may all be ours—but this one is mine."

As always, Vovka the rifleman showed up at just the right moment. He was a lot better than Rubakhin at both telling the truth and twisting it. "For us it's essential! Lay off! Gurov sent a note . . . It a chance for us to exchange prisoners!" He lied with true inspiration.

"But then you report it to the first lieutenant," someone said.

"It's already reported. Already agreed to!" Vovka went on, spilling words on top of words . . . that the lieutenant colonel was sitting at home drinking tea (which was true) and that the two of them had just come from there (also true), and Gurov, he says, personally signed the note for them. Yes, the note's there, at the checkpoint . . .

Vovka's face was noticeably shrunken. Rubakhin glanced at him with bewilderment: even though it was he who had raced through the brush in pursuit of the long-haired fighter, he who had caught and tied him up, he who had sweated it through, but Vovka was the one with the pale and hollow cheeks.

The prisoners (in formation at last) were led to the trucks. The weapons were carried separately. (Gurov will give the confiscated arms back to the guerrillas in exchange for food. A listless, nonstop war.) One of the soldiers took count aloud: seventeen Kalashnikovs, seven pistols, ten hand grenades. Two were killed during the chase, two were injured; the Russians also had one injury, and Kortkov was killed . . . The tarpaulin-covered trucks were lined up and escorted by two armored personnel carriers (at the head of the column and at the end), and picking up speed as they went, they headed to the unit with a din. In the trucks an excited discussion of the events got under way as the men bellowed back and forth at each other. They all wanted to eat.

As soon as they arrived, Rubakhin and Vovka quickly got out of the truck and broke away to the side with their prisoner. The others didn't pester them. Actually, there was nothing to be done with the prisoners: the young ones would be let go, the seasoned fighters would be held two or three months in the guardhouse, as a prison, but if they should try to escape, they would be shot, not without pleasure—it was war! Possibly these same warriors had killed

Boyarkov as he lay sleeping (or barely opening his sleepy eyes). His face had not the slightest scratch. And ants were crawling over it. At first Rubakhin and Vovka began raking off the ants. When they turned Boyarkov over, they found a hole piercing his back. The shots had been point-blank, but the bullets weren't spread out and had hit his chest in a cluster, smashing his rib cage. The bullets took out all his insides—on the ground (in the earth) lay a hash of ribs with the liver, kidneys, and rings of intestines on top, all in a big, cold pool of blood. Several bullets had come to rest within his still-steaming intestines. Boyarkov lay turned over with a huge gaping hole in his back. But his insides, mixed with bullets, lay in the earth.

Vovka turned off toward the dining hall.

"We got him for an exchange. The colonel gave permission," Vovka hastened to say, forestalling any questions from soldiers he met from Orlikov's platoon.

The soldiers, full after their meal, yelled out to him. "Tell 'em 'hi!'" Others asked, "Who got captured? Who're you trading for?"

"An exchange," Vovka the rifleman repeated.

Vanya Bravchenko laughed. "For hard currency!"

Sergeant Khodzhaev shouted, "Way to go, guys. Good you caught him. Those are the ones they love! Their boss . . . ," nodding toward the mountains, "really likes those kind."

Khodzhaev, himself from the Caucasus, laughed again, and to show what he meant he showed his strong, soldier's teeth.

"You'll be able to exchange two, three, maybe five for one!" he yelled. "Them kind—they love like a girl!" he added and winked as he drew abreast of Rubakhin.

Rubakhin stammered. He suddenly understood what it was that had bothered him about the captured fighter: the young man was beautiful.

He didn't speak Russian very well, but understood everything, of course.

Grudgingly, he spit out some high-pitched guttural sounds at Khodzhaev in reply to questions. When his face with its high cheekbones became flushed—framed by long dark hair falling to the shoulders almost in an oval—it became even more apparent that he was handsome. The shape of his lips. The fine line of the nose. The hazel eyes— large, slightly slanted and arched—especially caught and held a glance.

Vovka quickly came to an agreement with the cook. Before setting out, it was vital to have a good meal. It was noisy and stuffy at the long, rough-board table, and it was hot. They sat down at the end, and right on the spot Vovka extracted a half-finished bottle of sweet wine from his haver- sack; stealthily, he shoved it under the table to Rubakhin so that he could, as customary, grab it between his knees and drink it unnoticed by the others. "I left you an even half. Remember my generosity, Rubakha!"

He also set a plate in front of the prisoner.

"No want!" he replied sharply. Shaking his long thatch of hair, he turned away.

Vovka slid over closer to him. "At least take a little meat. It's a long haul."

The prisoner was silent. Vovka worried that he might push the plate away with his elbow and spill onto the floor the extra meat and kasha obtained from the cook with such difficulty.

He quickly divided this third portion between himself and Rubakhin. They ate. It was time to go.

5

They drank from the creek, the two soldiers taking turns at scooping water with a little plastic cup. The prisoner clearly was terribly thirsty; he rushed headlong to the stream and, scattering pebbles along the bank, seemed to collapse on his knees. He couldn't wait until they untied his hands or let him drink from the cup; bending forward on his knees to the swiftly flowing water, he drank for long time. His hands, tied behind his back for so long that they had turned blue, at the same time pitched upward; it seemed that he was praying in some unusual way.

Then he sat on the sand. His face was wet. Rubbing his cheek against his shoulder, he tried without the use of his hands to brush off the drops of water splattered across his face.

Rubakhin came over. "We would let you drink as much as you like. And would untie your hands . . . What's your hurry?"

He didn't answer. Rubakhin looked at him and with his hand wiped the water off his chin. The skin was so tender that Rubakhin's hand trembled. He hadn't anticipated it. But, yes, exactly. Like a girl's, he thought.

Their eyes met, and Rubakhin immediately averted his glance, suddenly embarrassed by some none-too-good thoughts that darted past.

For an instant the wind, rustling in the bushes, put Rubakhin on guard. Could it be someone's steps? . . . His embarrassment abated. (But it only concealed itself. It didn't completely leave.) Rubakhin was a simple soldier—he had no defense against human beauty as such. And here again it was as if a new and unfamiliar feeling was rising up within him by degrees. He also remembered of course that hoot and wink Sergeant Khodzhaev had given. Now a close face-to-face encounter lay in the offing. The prisoner couldn't cross the creek by himself. There was a bed of large stones and a swift current, and he was barefoot because his foot had swollen so at the ankle that at the very outset he'd had to take off his pretty tennis shoes (for now they were in Rubakhin's haversack). If he should fall a time or two crossing the creek, he could become totally useless. The creek would drag him away. There's no choice. And it's clear that Rubakhin—who else really?—had to carry him across the water: after all, wasn't it he who had injured his leg, since when trying to take him prisoner he had tossed his gun at him?

A feeling of compassion helped Rubakhin; compassion came to his aid at the right time and from somewhere above, as if out of the blue (but accompanied by another surge of embarrassment and, at the same time, a new understanding of the danger of this beauty). For just an instant, Rubakhin grew flustered. He seized the youth in his arms and started to carry him across the creek. The prisoner jerked, but Rubakhin's arms were powerful and strong.

"Now, now. Don't kick," he said, and they were approximately the same rather crude words that he would have said to a woman in a similar situation.

He carried him on and heard the youth's breathing. The latter turned his face away, but his hands (untied for the crossing) all the while clasped snugly around Rubakhin—certainly he didn't want to fall into the water, onto the rocks. Just like anyone else who's carrying a person in his arms, Rubakhin couldn't see anything underfoot and he stepped cautiously. Out of the corner of his eyes he could only see the far-off rushing waters of the creek, and against the background of cascading water, the youth's profile, tender, pure, with the unexpectedly puffed-out lower lip, stuck out willfully, like a young woman's.

Right here by the creek they made their first halt. For security they went downstream from the trail. They sat amid the bushes. Rubakhin held his automatic on his knees, with the safety off. They weren't hungry yet, but they drank water several times. Vovka, lying on his side, twisted the knobs of the little radio, which barely audibly squawked, burbled, mewed, exploded with unfamiliar speech. Vovka, just as always, relied on Rubakhin's experience—he could hear a rock under an outsider's foot from a kilometer away.

"Rubakha, I'm gonna sleep. Hear. I'm gonna sleep," he gave fair warning as he sunk into a momentary soldier's doze.

When the hawk-eyed first lieutenant had kicked him out of the squad selected for the raid, Vovka, having nothing else to do, went back to the little hut where the young woman lived. (The little shack was next to the home of the lieutenant colonel. But Vovka was careful.) Naturally, she told the soldier off, scolding him for so abruptly abandoning her at the store. But a minute later she was standing face to face with him, and within another minute they were in bed. So that now Vovka was pleasantly worn out. He could manage the hike, but at each halt he was overcome by a need to sleep.

It was easier for Rubakhin to start talking when they were moving briskly.

"In . . . normal times, what kind of enemies are we? We're brothers. We were truly friends! Can it be denied?" Rubakhin argued heatedly, even seemed to be insisting, yet hiding his troubled feelings within the typical (Soviet) words. And the feet just keep on moving.

Vovka the rifleman snorted, "Long live the indestructible friendship between peoples!"

Rubakhin heard, of course, the mockery. But he said with restraint, "Vov, I'm not talking to you."

Vovka in any case said no more. But the youth was silent, too.

"I'm the same kind of human being as you. And you're the same kind as me. What's the point of us fighting a war?" Rubakhin continued speaking words familiar to everyone, but off their mark; it turned out that he was speaking the trite words to himself and to the bushes all around. And also to the path that after the creek took off straight as an arrow into the mountains. Rubakhin would have liked for the youth to make some objection. Would have liked to hear his voice. For him to say something. (Rubakhin felt more and more uneasy.)

Vovka the rifleman (on the move) twirled a knob, and the little radio in his soldier's sack came to life, started to chirp.

Vovka gave it another spin—and found a marching song. But Rubakhin went on talking. Finally he got tired and fell silent.

To walk with hands tied (and with a bad foot) is not simple, if the climb is steep. The captured fighter fell behind; he was walking with difficulty. On one of the rises he suddenly fell. He awkwardly got back on his feet, he didn't complain; but Rubakhin noticed his tears.

A bit rashly Rubakhin said, "If you won't run away, I'll untie your hands. Give your word."

Vovka the rifleman heard (through the music from his radio) and shrieked, "Rubakha! Hey, you've gone off your rocker!"

Vovka was walking ahead. He swore. "Stupid thing to do." And the radio meanwhile played loudly.

"Vov. Turn it down! I need to hear."

"Just a second."

The music went silent.

Rubakhin untied the prisoner's hands—with a foot like that, how would he get away from him? From Rubakhin?

They moved pretty fast. The prisoner up ahead. Vovka, half-asleep, right behind. And a little behind, the silent Rubakhin, operating on instincts.

To free someone, even if just the wrists and only for a little while on the way, is gratifying. In sweet anticipation a lump of saliva formed in Rubakhin's throat. A rare moment. Despite the anticipation, his scrutiny didn't weaken. The path grew steeper. They went around the hillock where big drinker Boyarkov was buried. Bathed in evening sunlight, a splendid place.

At the night halt Rubakhin gave him his own wool socks. He himself stayed barefoot in his boots. They all needed to sleep! (And the campfire was quite small.) Rubakhin took Vovka's transistor away from him (not a sound at night). The automatic, as always, in his lap. He sat with his shoulder to the prisoner and his back against a tree, in his now long-

favored hunter's position (vigilant, but allowing a little dozing off). Night. He seemed to sleep. And in parallel to his
sleep he felt the prisoner sitting next to him—felt and sensed
him to such an extent that he would react instantaneously
should the other take it into his head to make even the
smallest irregular move. But he wasn't thinking at all of
escape. He was grieving. (Rubakhin delved into the other's
heart.) Then they both fell into a drowse (trusting), but
Rubakhin soon sensed that the youth became overwhelmed
with grief again. During the day the prisoner tried to bear
himself proudly, but now his inner pain was plainly wearing
him down. What in particular grieved him so? Even during
the day Rubakhin had distinctly hinted to him that they
weren't taking him to a military prison or for any other dark
purposes, but just to surrender him to his own men—in
exchange for a right to passage. That was the entire thing—
to hand him over to his people. Sitting next to Rubakhin, he
can relax. No need for him to know about the trucks and the
blocked road there, but for sure he knows (senses) that nothing is threatening him. Even more than that. He senses that
he, Rubakhin, sympathizes with him . . . Rubakhin suddenly felt uneasy again. Rubakhin glanced over sidelong. He was
grieving. In the now gathered darkness the face of the prisoner was beautiful as before and so sad. "Now, now!"
Rubakhin said in a friendly tone, trying to cheer him up.

And slowly stretched out a hand. Afraid of disturbing this
half-turn of the face and the startling beauty of the immobile
look, Rubakhin just slightly touched the fine cheekbone as
though straightening a lock of hair—a long strand which
curled along his cheek. The youth didn't turn his face aside.
He was silent. And as it seemed—but this could only seem
to be—barely perceptibly, his cheek responded to
Rubakhin's fingers.

Vovka the rifleman had only to shut his eyes and he was
reliving the fleeting sweet moments that had flown by

so furiously in that little country house. Moment after moment—separate and so brief—the joy of a woman's proximity. He slept sitting; he slept standing; he slept on the move. It's not surprising that at night he fell fast asleep (although it was his hour) and he didn't notice that nearby an animal ran past, possibly a boar. It stirred everybody up. And the crashing in the bushes continued a long time before fading away. "You want us also to be shot sleeping?" Rubakhin lightly jerked the soldier by the ear. He got up. He listened attentively. It was quiet.

Adding some brushwood to the fire, Rubakhin circled around the area a bit, stood a while at the canyon, returned. He sat down beside the prisoner. Having recovered from the scare, he was sitting rather tensely. The shoulders drooped; hunched over—the handsome face completely buried in the night. "Okay now? How about it?" he asked with the simplest words. In such situations a question is, first of all, a way of checking on the prisoner: Is his dozing a ruse? Was he trying to find a knife? And was he intending to slip away into the night while they slept? (A stupid thing to do—Rubakhin would catch him immediately.)

"Fine," he answered abruptly.

Both were silent for a while.

It turned out that after asking the questions, Rubakhin stayed sitting next to him (so as not to change his place by the fire every single minute).

Rubakhin patted him on the shoulder. "Don't be afraid. As I've said: soon as we get you there, we'll immediately hand you over to your people—understand?"

He nodded: yes, he understood. With a chuckle, Rubakhin said, "But you're handsome, no doubt about it."

They were silent again for a bit.

"How's the foot?"

"Okay."

"Fine, get some sleep. We've got just enough time. Gotta get a little more shut-eye, morning got here too fast . . . "

And right then, as if in agreement that to nap was necessary, the young captive slowly bent his head to the right, onto Rubakhin's shoulder. Nothing special: that's the way soldiers extend their short naps, leaning onto each other. But then the warmth of the body, and along with it, the flow of sensuality, too (also in separate waves), began to shoot through, flowing across—wave after wave—from the youth's leaning shoulder into Rubakhin's shoulder. No, of course not. The guy's sleeping. The guy's simply sleeping, Rubakhin thought, fending off a delusion. And at once he tensed up and stiffened—just at that moment a powerful surge of warmth and unexpected tenderness pierced his shoulder and entered his silenced inner thoughts. Rubakhin froze. And the youth—having sensed or guessed his guardedness—also keenly froze. Another minute—and their touching was rid of sensuality. They simply sat next to one another.

"Yes. Let's nap," said Rubakhin into nowhere. He spoke without taking his eyes off the small red tongues of the campfire.

The prisoner swayed, slightly more comfortably resting his head on Rubakhin's shoulder. And almost at once the flow of pliable and inviting warmth could again be felt. Rubakhin now began to sense the youth's quiet drowsing. "How can this be . . . what the devil is this?" he wondered, fully roused. And again he felt completely chilled and checked himself (and already fearing that a responsive shiver would give him away). But a shiver—after all, a mere shiver—can be endured. Most of all, Rubakhin feared that at any moment the youth's head would gently turn toward him (all his movements were gentle and palpably ingratiating, at the same time as seeming to be quite insignificant—a person stirred in his sleep, well, so what?)—would turn toward him, his face almost touching him, after which he would inevitably hear the youthful breathing and the nearness of the lips. The moment swelled. Rubakhin also experienced an instant's weakness. His stomach was the first of the bundle of organs to reject such an uncommon sensual overload—it contracted into a spasm, and instantly the abdominal muscles of the practiced soldier became as hard as a scrub board. And immediately he lost his breath. Rubakhin at once broke into a cough, and the youth, as if frightened, withdrew his head from Rubakhin's shoulder.

Vovka the rifleman woke up: "You're rumbling like a cannon. You lost your senses? You'd hear it half a kilometer away!"

Carefree Vovka immediately fell back to sleep. And himself—as a reply—started a slight snore. And with quite a resounding whistle at that.

Rubakhin burst into a laugh. "There," he says, "is my comrade-in-arms. Sleeps constantly. Sleeps in the daytime, sleeps at night!"

The prisoner said slowly and with a smile: "I think he had a woman. Yesterday."

Rubakhin was surprised. "Is that it?" And, recollecting, at once agreed. "Looks like it."

"I think yesterday during the day, it was."

"Right! Right!"

Both of them chuckled, as men often do in such situations.

But immediately (and very cautiously) the young prisoner asked, "And you—you had a woman long ago?"

Rubakhin shrugged. "Long ago. A year, say."

"Not pretty at all? Country woman? I think she was not pretty. Soldiers never have pretty women."

Such a long, uncomfortable silence arose. Rubakhin felt like a rock had lodged on the back of his head (and was weighing it down, down . . .).

In early morning the fire went out completely. Chilled to the bone, Vovka moved over with them and buried his head and shoulder in Rubakhin's back. The prisoner propped himself against Rubakhin to the side, all night luring the soldier with a sweet spot of warmth. So the three together, warming each other, made it to morning.

A pot with some water was set on the fire.

"We're indulging ourselves in tea," said Rubakhin with a certain sense of guilt from the unusual emotions of the night.

Right from the start of the morning, this sense of guilt, lacking self-confidence but now not able to conceal itself, came to life: Rubakhin suddenly began to look after the youth. (It worried him. He hadn't at all expected this from himself.) Like a malady, his hands impatiently sought little tasks. He twice brewed him some tea in a cup. He tossed in some lumps of sugar, stirred it up with a tinkling spoon, served it. He let him have his socks as if for keeps—"Wear them, don't take them off, you'll go farther in them!"—his concern showed itself in just this way.

And Rubakhin began bustling about and was constantly lighting the fire, lighting it so the prisoner would be warmer.

The prisoner drank the tea. He squatted and followed the movements of Rubakhin's hands.

"Warm socks. Good ones," he praised, shifting his glance to his own feet.

"My mother knitted them."

"O-oh."

"Don't take them off! As I said: you wear them. And I'll wrap something around my own feet."

The youth, getting a comb out of his pocket, busied himself with his hair: combed it for a long time. From time to time he proudly tossed his head. And again with meticulous strokes smoothed his hair out to his very shoulders. Feeling his own beauty was as natural to him as breathing the air.

In the warm and strong woolen socks the youth walked with a noticeably surer step. In fact, he acted more confident in every way. The sadness in his eyes was gone. He undoubtedly already knew that Rubakhin was embarrassed by the shape their relations had taken. Possibly this gratified him. He took side glances at Rubakhin, at his hands, at the automatic, and a smile would privately pass over his face, as if effortlessly he had gotten the upper hand over this enormous, strong, and shy young titan.

THE PRISONER FROM THE CAUSCASUS

At the creek he took off the socks. He stood waiting for Rubakhin to lift him up. The youth's hand didn't just grab hold of his collar as before; his soft hand freely held Rubakhin by the neck as he waded across the creek; at times, depending on how fast and firmly Rubakhin was stepping, he would slip his palm under the other's fatigue shirt, as a more comfortable hold.

Rubakhin again took the transistor away from Vovka. And signaled for silence: he was leading; on an extended, well-trod trail Rubakhin didn't trust anyone (not even the white rock face itself). The cliff whose forking of trails he knew well was already in sight. A dangerous place. But defended exactly because two narrow trails separated there (or joined, depending on the point of view).

The cliff (in the soldiers' simple term) was called *the nose*. A large white triangular ledge of rock loomed over them, like the nose of a ship—and stood hanging.

They were already clambering up the base, under the cliff itself, in the curly-leafed brush. *This can't be!* flashed through the soldier's mind when he heard up above the sound of something dangerous moving (both on the right and the left). Men were coming down both sides of the cliff. Hostile, and such a heavy, disorderly, but regular tread! *The bastards.* That two hostile detachments should coincide right to the minute like that, occupying both trails—*this can't be!* The cliff's saving grace was that by carrying the sound it allowed time to avoid an encounter.

Now, of course, they wouldn't have time to move away in any direction. Not even to scramble out from under the cliff and back into the woods through a clearing. There were three of them, one a prisoner; they would be immediately noticed; they would be fired on at once; or simply driven into a thicket and surrounded. *This can't be*—for the third time the thought screeched through his mind, in plaintive denial. (Then it left— disappeared, abandoned him.) Now everything was by instinct. A chill pinched his nostrils. Not only their steps. In the almost completely still air Rubakhin heard a slow parting of the grass as they began passing.

"Ss-hhh."

He pressed a finger to his lips. Vovka understood. And nodded toward the prisoner: what about him?

Rubakhin glanced into his face: the youth also instantly understood (understood that his own men were coming), his forehead and cheeks slowly flushed—a sign of unpredictable behavior.

"Ah! Whatever—let it happen!" Rubakhin said to himself, quickly readying his automatic for battle. He felt his belt for extra clips. But the thought of battle (just like any thought in an instant of danger) also moved aside (abandoned him), not wishing to take an answer upon itself. Instinct demanded keen attention. And waiting. A chill pinched his nostrils again and again. And the grass quietly, meaningfully rustled. The steps were closer. No. There're many of them. Too many . . . Glancing again at the prisoner's face, Rubakhin tried to calculate and guess—what about him? What's he thinking? Would he freeze up from fear of being killed and keep silent (that would be good) or would he at the first moment rush out joyfully to meet them, with the look of a maniac reflected in his half-crazed, enormous eyes, and (mainly!) would he shout?

Without taking his eyes off the men moving along the trail on the left (this detachment was quite close and would pass by them first), Rubakhin reached his arm back and cautiously touched the body of the prisoner, who trembled slightly, as a woman trembles before a close embrace. Rubakhin touched his neck, then by feel shifted over to his face, and touching lightly, placed his fingers and palm on the beautiful lips, on the mouth (which must be silent); the lips trembled.

Rubakhin slowly drew the youth closer to him (his eyes on the left trail, on the detachment moving up in a file). Vovka kept watch on the detachment to the right: steps could be heard from there, too, gravel slipped below, and one of the fighters with an automatic on his shoulder kept clanking it against the weapon of the man walking behind him.

The prisoner didn't resist Rubakhin, who, taking him by the shoulder, turned him around toward himself—the youth himself (he was standing slightly below) even drew toward him, pressed closer, sticking his lips below his unshaven chin into the carotid artery. The youth was shaking, not understanding. "N-n . . . ," he weakly breathed out, quite like a woman who has pronounced her "no" not as a refusal, but as an expression of modesty, at the same time as Rubakhin watched him and waited (guarding against a shriek). And similarly wide-eyed, trying in fear to avoid meeting Rubakhin's eyes, and—through air and sky—catch sight of his own men! He opened his mouth, yet still didn't shout. Maybe all he wanted was to grab a deep breath of air. But with the other hand Rubakhin put his automatic down on the ground and covered both the slightly opened mouth with its beautiful lips and the nose, which was slightly quivering. "N-nuh . . . " The youthful prisoner wanted to say something, but didn't have time. His body jerked, legs stiffened, although now unsupported. Rubakhin swept him off the ground. He held him in an embrace to prevent his feet from touching either a sensitive bush or rocks that might stir and make a sound. Blocking any vision, Rubakhin circled the neck with the hand that embraced him. He squeezed; no, beauty didn't manage to save. Several convulsions . . . and that's all.

Quite soon, lower down the cliff where the trails joined, friendly, guttural-sounding shouts echoed. The detachments had discovered each other. Greetings could be heard, and questions: How? What! Where are you headed? (The most likely of questions.) Slaps on each other's shoulders. Laughing. One of the fighters, making use of the halt, decided to relieve himself. He ran up to the cliff, which provided a convenient spot. He didn't know that he was already sighted in crosshairs. He stood just several steps away from the bushes that concealed two live men (they lay down and hid low) and a dead one. He finished, hiccuped, and, hitching up his pants, rushed off.

When the detachments passed by and were moving into the distance below, and their steps and voices had faded totally away, the two soldiers with automatics dragged the body out of the bushes. They carried him into the sparse woods not far away, by the trail on the left, where, as Rubakhin remembered, there was a clearing—a dry, bald patch with sandy, moist earth. They dug a hole, scooping the sand out with flat rocks. Vovka the rifleman asked whether Rubakhin was going to take his socks back; Rubakhin shook his head. And not a word about the person that, all in all, they had gotten accustomed to. They sat down in silence for half a minute beside the grave. Sit a while? No way—there's a war on!

6

No change: two cargo trucks (Rubakhin sees them from far away) are standing in the same spot.

The road squeezes itself without a break into a passage between cliffs, but guerrillas guard the narrow corridor. The trucks are already shot up with bullet holes, but with random aim. (If you move closer, you see twice as many—simply riddled.) The trucks are sitting there for the fourth day, waiting. The guerrillas want arms—then they'll let them through.

"We're not carrying automatics! We got no weapons!" comes a shout from the truck side. A shot from the cliff rings in reply. Or a whole volley of shots, in a long series. And as added fillip, laughter—*ha-ha-ha-ha!*—such joyful, bubbling laughter, so gloatingly childlike, rolls down from the heights.

The soldier escorts and drivers (six people altogether) have taken up a position by the bushes on the roadside, sheltered by the truck bodies. Their nomadic life is simple: they're either cooking food on the campfire or sleeping.

When Rubakhin and Vovka the rifleman get closer on the cliff to the area of the siege, Rubakhin spots a fire, a pale, daytime campfire—the guerrillas are also cooking dinner. It's a slack war. Why not chow down till you're stuffed, why not drink hot tea?

As they draw ever closer, Rubakhin and Vovka are also noticed from the cliff. The guerrillas are sharp-sighted. And although it's apparent that the pair had returned just as they had left (carrying nothing visible), shots ring out from the cliff, just in case. One round. Another round.

Rubakhin and Vovka had already reached their own men.

The sergeant major juts his stomach out. "Well? Any support coming?" he asks Rubakhin.

"Not a fuckin' thing!" Rubakhin didn't try to explain.

"And you didn't manage to trap a prisoner?"

"Nope."

Rubakhin asked for some water and drank from the bucket for a long time, pouring it straight onto his fatigue shirt, onto his chest, then blindly strode to the side, and without caring where he was, collapsed in the bushes to sleep. The grass was still bent flat—it was the same spot where he had been lying two days before when he got poked in the ribs and sent to get help (and was given Vovka in the bargain). He stuck his head into the soft grass up to his ears, not hearing the sergeant major's reproaches. He didn't give a shit. He was tired.

Vovka sat down beside a tree, stretched his legs out, and pulled a straw hat over his eyes. He asked the drivers sarcastically, "What's wrong? You guys couldn't do it? Didn't find a detour? You don't mean it!"

"There is no detour," they answered him. The drivers were lying in the tall grass. One of these slow-witted types was rolling his own cigarette from a scrap of newspaper.

Sergeant Major Beregevoy, irked by the mission's failure, again tried to engage in some negotiations.

"Hey," he yelled. "Hear me! Hey!" he yelled in a trusting

(as he considered it) voice. "I swear, there's nothing of the kind in the trucks—no weapons, no food. We're empty! Let one of your men come and check—we'll show you, we won't shoot him. Hey! Listen!"

Shots resounded in response. And boisterous laughter.

"Up your mother's!" the sergeant major swore.

Shots came from the cliff erratically. The shooting went on so long and so senselessly that the sergeant major let out another oath and called out, "Vov! Vov! Come here. Show the *abreks** how to shoot!"

Vovka the rifleman yawned; he lazily removed his back from the tree trunk. (He was sitting so nicely as to be anchored to it.)

But the laziness disappeared once he grabbed his weapon and aimed. He took up a comfortable position on the grass, and thrusting his carbine out, he fixed the sight on one, then another of the silhouettes that flitted about on the cliff, to the left above the road. They were all clearly visible. Maybe he could hit the target even without the optical sight.

Just at that moment a mountaineer standing on the edge of the cliff let out a whoop, like a taunt.

"Vov. Wouldn't you like to hit him?" asked a driver.

"I say to hell with him," snorted Vovka.

He paused, then added, "I like to aim and squeeze the trigger. I know when I hit even without the bullet."

The impossibility was clear without words: kill even one fighter and the trucks for sure won't pass down this road.

"Just consider that I zapped that one! And I can rip half this one's ass off. Not kill him—he's behind a tree—but half his ass—easy!"

At times, if he saw one of the mountaineers with something that flashed in the sun—a bottle of vodka or (as there was in the morning!) an excellent Chinese thermos, Vovka

---

* *Abrek*—Ossetian word for mountain warrior, used frequently in Russian literature of the Caucasus.

would carefully aim and shatter the visible object to smith-ereens. But now there was nothing that attracted the eye.

In the meantime, Rubakhin's sleep was restless. The same stupid, disturbing dream broke in (or, burying himself in the grass, Rubakhin himself called it up): the beautiful face of the youthful prisoner.

"Vovk'. Gimme a smoke!" (And what kind of pleasure is it to catch one of them through the crosshairs?)

"Just a second!" Vovka aimed again and again, all absorbed in his game—he aimed the sight on one or another of the cliff's silhouettes: the outline of a rock . . . a mountain bush . . . a tree trunk. O-ho! He noticed a gaunt fighter; standing by a tree, he was bobbing off his long hair. A haircut is something intimate. The little mirror flashed, giving a signal—Vovka in a instant loaded and aimed. He pressed the trigger and the silvery little pool that had been fastened to the trunk of an elm exploded into tiny pieces. Oaths resounded in reply and, as always, random firing. (As if cranes had broken out honking beyond the cliff that hung over the road: *gulyal-kilyal-lyal—kilyal-sniper* . . .) The silhouettes on the cliff began running—shouted, shrieked, whooped. But after that (obviously on a command), fell silent. For a certain time they didn't show themselves (and generally their behavior was more subdued). And they thought, of course, that they were hidden from sight. Vovka the rifleman not only saw their concealed heads, their Adam's apples, their stomachs—he also saw the buttons of their shirts, and continuing to play, he drew the crosshairs across from one button to another . . .

"Vovka! Cut it out!" the sergeant major admonished.

"Right!" responded the rifleman, taking the carbine and heading toward the tall grass (with a soldier's usual simple thought: catch some sleep).

But Rubakhin kept losing focus: the youth's face held only briefly before his eyes—the face fell apart almost as soon as it emerged. It washed away, losing itself and leaving only an indistinct and dull prettiness. Someone's face. Forgotten. The image melted. As if in farewell (parting and, maybe, forgiving him) the youth again acquired more or less clear features (and how it shone!). The face. But not only the face—the youth himself stood. It seemed that he was about to say something. He stepped even closer and abruptly grabbed Rubakhin by the neck with his arms (as Rubakhin had done on that cliff), but his slender arms turned out to be soft, like a young woman's—jerky, but tender, and Rubakhin (he was on guard) managed to grasp that right then in his dream a certain male weakness could occur. He ground his teeth, with effort driving the vision away, and then woke up, feeling an aching heaviness in his groin.

"If I could have a smoke!" he muttered hoarsely. And heard the firing . . .

Possibly the shots even woke him up. The thin stream of an automatic round—*tuk-tuk-tuk-tuk-tuk*—kicked up light gravel and little curls of dust on the road by the idle trucks. The trucks sat there. (This didn't bother Rubakhin much. At some point, sure, the road will be opened for them.)

Vovka the rifleman slept in the grass nearby, with his rifle in his arms. Vovka had some strong cigarettes now (bought, together with the sweet wine, in the little village store)—the cigarettes were visible, sticking out of his breast pocket. Rubakhin fished one out. Vovka snuffled lightly in his sleep.

Rubakhin smoked, taking slow draws. He was lying on his back —looking up at the sky, but crowding in from the left and the right (pressing on his peripheral vision) were those same mountains that surrounded him here and wouldn't let him go. Rubakhin had served his time. Every time that he got ready to say to hell with everything and everyone (and go home for good, to the steppe across the Don), he hastily got out his battered suitcase and . . . and stayed. "So what's so special here? The mountains?" he muttered aloud, with wrath not at someone else, but at himself. "What's so interesting in the coldness of the army barracks—in fact, what's so interesting in the mountains themselves?" he thought with annoyance. He wanted to add, "How many years now!" But instead he said, "How many centuries now!" As if by a slip of the tongue, the words jumped out of a shadow, and the soldier, surprised, pondered this quiet thought that had settled into the depth of his consciousness. Gray, mossy gorges. Poor and shabby little houses of the mountain people, stuck together like birds' nests. But still—the mountains! Their peaks, yellow in the sun, crowd together all around. Mountains. Mountains. Mountains. How long now have their majesty, their mute solemnity chafed his heart—but what actually did their beauty want to say to him? Why did it call?

June–September 1994